On the table **──────** a
large candleh███████ ██ █████ █ █████
of candles burned brightly.

Señor Zorro sprang toward it. With
one sweep of his hand, he dashed it to
the floor, extinguishing all the candles
in an instant and plunging the room
into darkness.

He evaded the wild rush of Don
Carlos, springing across the room so
lightly that his soft boots made not the
slightest noise. For an instant, Señorita
Lolita felt a man's arm around her waist,
gently squeezing it, felt a man's breath
on her cheek, and heard a man's
whisper in her ear:

"Until later, señorita."

Don Carlos was bellowing like a
bull to direct the soldiers to the scene.
Already some of them were pounding
at the front door. Señor Zorro rushed
from the room and into the kitchen.
The servants fled before him as if he
were a ghost. . . .

A Background Note about
The Mark of Zorro

Johnston McCulley blends elements from three different periods of early California history to create the backdrop for *The Mark of Zorro*. Up until 1821, Spain ruled the area. During this time, they built military bases (presidios) and stationed soldiers in the area. At the same time, the Spanish clergy established more than twenty missions along the coast. These were vast estates run by Jesuit and Franciscan friars. Their purpose was to convert and control the Native Americans.

When Mexico took control of California, the missions were taken away from the church. The land was given to wealthy aristocrats—men of "good blood." These men turned the missions into haciendas—vast private estates. These gentlemen and their sons were the caballeros.

After California came under the control of the United States in 1848, the Mexicans living there were often cheated and persecuted. During this period, some Mexicans became bandits who defended the poor. They stole from the rich and punished those who abused Mexicans or Native Americans. In other words, they were men much like Señor Zorro.

Johnston McCulley

The Mark of ZORRO

Edited, and with an Afterword,
by Bill Blauvelt

 THE TOWNSEND LIBRARY

THE MARK OF ZORRO

TP THE TOWNSEND LIBRARY

For more titles in the Townsend Library,
visit our website: **www.townsendpress.com**

All new material in this edition is
copyright © 2007 by Townsend Press.
Printed in the United States of America

0 9 8 7 6 5 4 3 2 1

ISBN 13: 978-1-59194-071-5
ISBN 10: 1-59194-071-0

Library of Congress Control Number:
2006926042

CONTENTS

1. Pedro, the Boaster 1
2. On the Heels of the Storm 8
3. Señor Zorro Pays a Visit 16
4. Swords Clash—And Pedro Explains . 21
5. A Ride in the Morning 31
6. Diego Seeks a Bride 37
7. A Different Sort of Man 46
8. Don Carlos Plays a Game 54
9. The Clash of Blades 63
10. A Hint of Jealousy 73
11. Three Suitors 81
12. A Visit 89
13. Love Comes Swiftly 100
14. Captain Ramón Writes a Letter 112
15. At the Presidio 117
16. The Chase that Failed 127
17. Sergeant Gonzales Meets a Friend ... 134
18. Don Diego Returns 141
19. Captain Ramón Apologizes 146
20. Don Diego Shows Interest 154
21. The Whipping 159
22. Swift Punishment 165
23. More Punishment 171

24. At the Hacienda of Don Alejandro . . 178
25. A League Is Formed 188
26. An Understanding 194
27. Orders for Arrest 203
28. The Outrage 211
29. Don Diego Feels Ill 220
30. The Sign of the Fox 228
31. The Rescue 233
32. Close Quarters 241
33. Flight and Pursuit 251
34. The Blood of the Pulidos 258
35. The Clash of Blades Again 264
36. All Against Them 279
37. The Fox at Bay 285
38. The Man Unmasked 291
39. "Meal Mush and Goat's Milk!" 298
    Afterword 302

CHAPTER 1

Pedro, the Boaster

Again the sheet of rain beat against the roof of red Spanish tile and the wind shrieked like a soul in torment. Smoke puffed from the big fireplace as the sparks were showered over the hard dirt floor.

"It's a night for evil deeds!" declared Sergeant Pedro Gonzales, grasping the hilt of his sword in one hand and a mug filled with thin wine in the other. He stretched his great feet in their loose boots toward the roaring fire and continued, "Devils howl in the wind, and demons are in the raindrops! It is an evil night, indeed— eh, señor?"

"It is!" The fat landlord agreed. And he quickly filled the wine mug again, for Sergeant Pedro Gonzales had a terrible temper that was always aroused when wine was too slow in coming.

"An evil night," the big sergeant repeated, and drained the mug without stopping to draw breath. This feat had gained the sergeant a certain reputation up and down El Camino Real, as they called the highway that connected the missions in one long chain.

Gonzales sprawled closer to the fire. He did not care that he robbed other men of some of its warmth. Sergeant Pedro Gonzales often had expressed his belief that a man should look out for his own comfort before considering others. Being of great size and strength, and having great skill with the sword, he found few who had the courage to contradict him.

Outside the wind shrieked, and the rain dashed against the ground in a solid sheet. It was a typical February storm for southern California. At the missions the friars—the religious brothers—had cared for the stock and had closed the buildings for the night. At every great hacienda big fires were burning in the houses. The Indians kept to their little adobe huts, glad for shelter.

And here in the village, the little pueblo of Reina de Los Angeles, where, in years to come, a great city would grow, the tavern stood on one side of the plaza. Tonight it housed men who would sprawl before the fire until the dawn rather than face the beating rain.

Sergeant Pedro Gonzales hogged the fireplace. A corporal and three soldiers from the military post—the presidio—sat at table behind him, drinking their thin wine and playing at cards. An Indian servant crouched on his heels in one corner.

Just now conversation had died out. This fact annoyed the fat landlord and caused him some

fear there would be trouble. He knew that Sergeant Pedro Gonzales in an argument was Sergeant Gonzales at peace. If the sergeant was not arguing, he might feel moved to action and start a brawl.

Twice before Gonzales had done so, to the great damage of furniture and men's faces. When the landlord had complained to the commandant of the presidio, Captain Ramón, he got no help. Captain Ramón had replied that running the tavern was the landlord's problem, not the captain's.

So the landlord cautiously watched Gonzales. Edging closer to the long table, he spoke in an attempt to start a general conversation and so head off trouble.

"They are saying in the pueblo," he announced, "that this Señor Zorro has appeared again."

His words had an unexpected effect. Sergeant Pedro Gonzales hurled his half-filled wine mug to the hard dirt floor and crashed his huge fist down on the table, causing wine mugs and cards to scatter in all directions.

The corporal and the three soldiers retreated a few feet in fright. The red face of the landlord turned pale. The Indian sitting in the corner started to creep toward the door, preferring the storm outside to the big sergeant's anger.

"Señor Zorro, eh?" Gonzales cried in a terrible voice. "Must I always hear that name? Señor Zorro, eh? Mr. Fox, in other words! He imagines, I take it, that he is as cunning as one. By the saints, he makes as much trouble as a fox!"

Gonzales turned to face the others and continued his tirade.

"He runs up and down the length of El Camino Real like a goat of the high hills! He wears a mask, and he flashes a pretty blade, they tell me. He uses the point of it to carve his hated letter Z on the cheek of his foe! Ha! The mark of Zorro they are calling it! But Señor Zorro will not do me the honor of letting me see his flashing sword! His sly attacks never occur in the vicinity of Sergeant Pedro Gonzales! Perhaps this Señor Zorro can tell us the reason for that? Ha!"

He glared at the men before him.

"They are calling him the Curse of Capistrano now," the fat landlord observed, stooping to pick up the wine mug and cards.

"Curse of the entire highway and the whole mission chain!" Sergeant Gonzales roared. "A cutthroat, he is! A thief! Ha! A common fellow trying to get him a reputation for bravery because he robs a hacienda or so and frightens a few women! Señor Zorro, eh? Here is one fox it gives me pleasure to hunt! Curse of Capistrano, eh? I know I have led an evil life, but I only ask of the saints one thing now—that they forgive me my sins long enough to let me stand face to face with this pretty highwayman!"

"There is a reward—" the landlord began.

"You snatch the very words from my lips!" Sergeant Gonzales growled. "There is a pretty reward for the fellow's capture, offered by his excellency the governor. And what good fortune has come to my blade? I am away on duty at San Juan Capistrano, and the fellow makes his play at Santa Barbara. I am at Reina de Los Angeles, and he takes a fat purse at San Diego de Alcala! A pest, he is! Once I met him—"

Sergeant Gonzales reached for the wine mug, which the landlord had filled again and placed at his elbow. He gulped down the contents.

"Well, he never has visited us here," the landlord said with a sigh of relief.

"Good reason, fat one! We have a presidio here and a few soldiers. He keeps far away from any military post, does this pretty Señor Zorro!

He is like a fleeting sunbeam—and with about as much real courage!"

Sergeant Gonzales relaxed on the bench again. The landlord looked and began to hope that there would be no broken mugs and furniture this rainy night.

"Yet this Señor Zorro must rest at times—he must eat and sleep," the landlord said. "He must have some hiding place. Some fine day the soldiers will trail him to his den."

"Ha!" Gonzales replied. "Of course the man has to eat and sleep. And you know what he claims now? He says that he is no real thief, by the saints! He is just punishing those who mistreat the men of the missions, he says. Friend of the oppressed, eh? He left a note at Santa Barbara recently stating as much, did he not? Ha! The friars of the missions are shielding him, hiding him, giving him his meat and drink! Shake down a robed friar and you'll find some trace of this pretty highwayman's whereabouts!"

"I have no doubt that you speak the truth," the landlord replied. "I wouldn't put it past the friars to do such a thing. But may this Señor Zorro never visit us here!"

"And why not, fat one?" Sergeant Gonzales cried in a voice of thunder. "Am I not here? Have I not a sword at my side? By the saints—"

"I mean," said the landlord quickly, "that I have no wish to be robbed."

"To be—robbed of what, fat one? Of a jug of weak wine and a meal? Have you riches, fool? Ha! Let this bold and cunning Señor Zorro but enter that door and step before us! Let him bow, as they say he does, and let his eyes twinkle through his mask! Let me but face the fellow for an instant—and I will claim the generous reward offered by his excellency!"

"He perhaps is afraid to come so near the presidio," the landlord said.

"More wine!" Gonzales howled. "More wine, fat one, and place it to my account! When I have earned the reward, you shall be paid in full. I promise it on my word as a soldier! Ha! If only this brave and cunning Señor Zorro, this Curse of Capistrano, were to step through that door now—" The door suddenly was opened!

CHAPTER 2

On the Heels of the Storm

In came a gust of wind and rain and a man with it. The candles flickered, and one went out. This sudden entrance startled them all. Gonzales drew his sword halfway from its scabbard as his words died in his throat. The Indian quickly closed the door again to keep out the wind.

The newcomer turned and faced them. The landlord gave another sigh of relief. It was not Señor Zorro, of course. It was Don Diego Vega, a handsome young man from an important family. He was twenty-four and was known the length of El Camino Real for his lack of interest in the really important things of life.

"Ha!" Gonzales cried, and slammed his sword back into its scabbard.

Don Diego glanced around the big room and nodded to the men before him. "Did I startle you, señores?" he asked politely and in a thin voice.

"If you did, señor, it was because you entered on the heels of the storm," the sergeant replied.

8

"Your own energy is not enough to startle any man."

"Hm!" grunted Don Diego, throwing aside his sombrero and flinging off his soaked serape. "Your remarks border on insulting, my rowdy friend."

"Can it be that you intend to make me pay for my remarks?"

"It is true," continued Don Diego, "that I do not have a reputation for riding like a fool at risk of my neck, fighting like an idiot with every newcomer, and playing the guitar under every woman's window like a simpleton. I know you think of these things as shortcomings. Nevertheless, I do not care to have them thrown in my face."

"Ha!" Gonzales cried, half in anger.

"We have an agreement, Sergeant Gonzales, that we can be friends. I can forget the wide difference in birth and breeding that yawns between us only as long as you curb your tongue and stand as my comrade. Your boasts amuse me, and in exchange I buy you wine—it is a pretty arrangement. But if you make fun of me again, señor, either in public or private, then the agreement is at an end. I may mention that I have some small influence—"

"Your pardon, caballero and my very good friend!" the alarmed Sergeant Gonzales cried. "There's no need to get angry just because my tongue happened to slip. From now on, if any man asks, you are quick with a blade and always ready to fight or to make love. You are a man of action, caballero! Ha! Does any dare doubt it?"

He glared around the room, half drawing his blade again. Then he slammed the sword home, roared with laughter, and slapped Don Diego on the back. The fat landlord hurried with more wine, knowing that Don Diego Vega would pay the bill.

This peculiar friendship between Don Diego and Sergeant Gonzales was the talk of El Camino Real. Don Diego came from a family of noble blood that ruled over thousands of broad acres, countless herds of horses and cattle, great fields of grain. Don Diego, in his own right, had a hacienda that was like a small empire, and a house in the pueblo also. And he would inherit from his father more than three times what he had now.

But Don Diego was unlike the other young nobles—the caballero—of the times. It appeared that he disliked action. He seldom wore his sword, except as a matter of style. He was extremely polite to all women yet he courted none.

He sat in the sun and listened to the wild tales of other men—and now and then he smiled. He was the opposite of Sergeant Pedro Gonzales in all things, and yet they were together frequently. It was as Don Diego had said—he enjoyed the sergeant's boasts, and the sergeant enjoyed the free wine. What more could either ask in the way of a fair arrangement?

Now Don Diego went to stand before the fire and dry himself, holding a mug of red wine in one hand. He was only medium in size, but he was healthy and good-looking. All of the proud duennas thought he would make a fine husband for the daughters they protected. But, to their sorrow, he would not give a second glance at the pretty señoritas.

Gonzales was afraid that he had angered his friend and that the free wine would be at an end. He was anxious to make peace.

"Caballero, we have been speaking of this notorious Señor Zorro—this fine Curse of Capistrano, as some fool has seen fit to name the pest."

"What about him?" Don Diego asked, putting down his wine mug and hiding a yawn behind his hand.

"I have been remarking, caballero," said the sergeant, "that this fine Señor Zorro never appears in my vicinity. I am hoping the good saints will grant me the chance of facing him some fine day. Then I can claim the reward offered by the governor. Señor Zorro, eh? Ha!"

"Let us not speak of him," Don Diego begged, turning from the fireplace. "Must the talk always be of bloodshed and violence? Would it be possible in these turbulent times for a man to listen to words of wisdom regarding music or the poets?"

"Meal mush and goat's milk!" snorted Sergeant Gonzales in disgust. "If this Señor Zorro wishes to risk his neck, let him. It is his own neck, by the saints! A cutthroat! A thief! Ha!"

"I have heard much about his work," Don Diego went on to say. "No doubt, the fellow is sincere in his purpose. The only people he has robbed are officials who have stolen from the missions and the poor. And the only people he has punished are brutes who mistreat Indians. He has killed no one, I understand. Let him have his little day of fame, my sergeant."

"I would rather have the reward!"

"Earn it," Don Diego said. "Capture the man!"

"Ha! Dead or alive, the governor's proclamation says. I myself have read it."

"Then stand you up to him and run him through, if it pleases you," Don Diego replied. "And tell me all about it afterward—but spare me now."

"It will be a pretty story!" Gonzales cried. "And you shall have it entire, caballero, word by word! How I played with him, how I laughed at him as we fought, how I pressed him back after a time and ran him through—"

"Afterward—but not now!" Don Diego cried, exasperated. "Landlord, more wine! The only manner in which to stop this noisy boaster is to make his wide throat so slick with wine that the words cannot climb out of it!"

The landlord quickly filled the mugs. Don Diego sipped at his wine slowly, as a gentleman should. Sergeant Gonzales took his in two great gulps. Then the son of the house of Vega stepped to the bench and reached for his sombrero and his serape.

"What?" the sergeant cried. "You are leaving us at such an early hour, caballero? You are going to face the fury of that beating storm?"

"At least I am brave enough for that," Don Diego replied, smiling. "I only ran over from my house for a pot of honey. Get me one, landlord."

"I shall escort you safely home through the rain!" Sergeant Gonzales cried. He knew full well that Don Diego had excellent wine there.

"You shall remain here before the roaring fire," Don Diego told him firmly. "I do not need an escort of soldiers from the presidio to cross the plaza. I am going over accounts with my secretary. I may return to the tavern after we have finished. I wanted the pot of honey that we might eat as we worked."

"Ha! And why did you not send that secretary of yours for the honey, caballero? Why be wealthy and have servants, if a man cannot send them on errands on such a stormy night?"

"He is an old man and feeble," Don Diego explained. "He also is secretary to my aged father. The storm would kill him. Landlord, serve everyone here with wine and put it on my bill. I may return when my books have been straightened out."

Don Diego Vega picked up the pot of honey, wrapped his serape around his head, opened the door, and plunged into the storm and darkness.

"There goes a fine man!" Gonzales cried. "He is my friend, that caballero, and I would have all men know it! He seldom wears a sword, and I doubt whether he can use one—but he is my friend! Music and the poets, eh? Ha! Has he not the right, if such is his pleasure? Is he not Don Diego Vega? Has he not blue blood? He may do as he pleases. And he is my friend!"

The fat landlord served them with another round since Don Diego would pay. The landlord knew it was beneath a Vega to look at his bill in a public tavern, and he had taken advantage of this fact many times.

"If only," Sergeant Gonzales continued, "I had his youth and good looks and riches—Ha! There would be a stream of broken hearts from San Diego de Alcala to San Francisco de Asis!"

"And broken heads!" the corporal offered.

"Ha! And broken heads, comrade! I would rule the country! No youngster should stand long in my way. Out with blade and at them! Cross Pedro Gonzales, eh? Ha! Through the shoulder—neatly! Ha! Through a lung!"

Gonzales was on his feet now, his sword in his hand. He swept it back and forth through the air, thrust, parried, lunged, advanced, and retreated, shouted his oaths, and roared his laughter as he fought with shadows.

"What have we here?" he screeched at the fireplace. "Two of you against one? So much the better, señores! Ha! Have at you, dog! Die, hound! One side, coward!"

He reeled against the wall, gasping, his breath almost gone. The point of his blade rested on the floor, his great face was purple with the exertion and the wine he had consumed. And the corporal and the soldiers and the fat landlord laughed long and loudly at this bloodless battle from which Sergeant Pedro Gonzales had emerged the unquestioned victor.

"If only this fine Señor Zorro was before me here and now!" the sergeant gasped.

And again the door was opened suddenly, and a man entered the inn on a gust of the storm.

CHAPTER 3

Señor Zorro Pays a Visit

The Indian hurried forward to fasten the door against the force of the wind, and then retreated to his corner again. The newcomer had his back toward those in the long room. His sombrero was pulled far down on his head. His body was wrapped in a long dark cloak that was wringing wet.

With his back still toward them, he opened the cloak and shook the raindrops from it and then closed it around himself again. The fat landlord hurried forward, rubbing his hands together in expectation. He guessed that here was some caballero off the highway who would pay good money for food and bed and care of his horse.

When the landlord was within a few feet of him, the stranger whirled around. The landlord gave a little cry of fear and quickly retreated. The corporal gurgled deep down in his throat. The soldiers gasped. Sergeant Pedro Gonzales allowed his lower jaw to drop and let his eyes bulge.

For the man who stood straight before them had a black mask over his face that concealed his features. Through the two slits in it his eyes glittered ominously.

"Ha! What have we here?" Gonzales gasped finally.

The man before them bowed.

"Señor Zorro, at your service," he said.

"By the saints! Señor Zorro, eh?" Gonzales cried.

"Do you doubt it, señor?"

"If you are indeed Señor Zorro, then have you lost your wits!" the sergeant declared.

"Why would you say that?"

"You are here, are you not? You have entered the inn, have you not? By all the saints, you have walked into a trap, my pretty highwayman!"

"Will the señor please explain?" Señor Zorro asked. His voice was deep.

"Are you blind? Are you without sense?" Gonzales demanded. "Am I not here?"

"And what has that to do with it?"

"Am I not a soldier?"

"At least you wear a soldier's uniform, señor."

"By the saints, and cannot you see the good corporal and three of our comrades? Have you come to surrender your wicked sword, señor? Are you finished playing at rogue?"

Señor Zorro laughed, but he did not take his

eyes from Gonzales.

"Most certainly I have not come to surrender," he said. "I am on business, señor."

"Business?" Gonzales asked.

"Four days ago, señor, you brutally beat an Indian who had annoyed you. It happened on the road between here and the mission at San Gabriel."

"He was a worthless dog and got in my way! And how does it concern you, my pretty highwayman?"

"I am the friend of the oppressed, señor, and I have come to punish you."

"Come to—to punish me, fool? You punish me? I shall die of laughter before I can run you through! You are as good as dead, Señor Zorro! His excellency has offered a pretty price for your carcass! If you are a religious man, say your prayers! I would not have it said that I killed a man without giving him time to repent his crimes. I give you the space of a hundred heartbeats."

"You are generous, Señor, but there is no need for me to say my prayers."

"Then must I do my duty," said Gonzales, and lifted the point of his blade. "Corporal, you will remain by the table, and the men also. I do not want to share the reward for this man!"

He advanced carefully. He had heard of this man's skill with a blade and he did not want to underestimate his foe. And when he was within the proper distance he jumped back suddenly, as if a snake had warned of a strike.

Señor Zorro had allowed one hand to come from beneath his cloak, and the hand held a pistol.

"Back, señor!" the masked man warned.

"Ha! So that is your method!" Gonzales cried. "You carry that devil's weapon and threaten men with it! Such things are for use only at a long distance and against inferior foes. Gentlemen prefer the trusty blade."

"Back, señor! There is death in this you call the devil's weapon. I will not warn again."

"Somebody told me you were a brave man," Gonzales taunted, retreating a few feet. "It has been whispered that you would meet any man foot to foot and cross blades with him. I have believed it of you. And now I find you resorting to a weapon fit for nothing except to use against Indians. Can it be, señor, that you lack the courage I have heard you possess?"

Señor Zorro laughed again.

"As to that, you shall see soon enough," he said. "This pistol is necessary at the present time. I find myself pitted against large odds in this tavern, señor. I will cross blades with you gladly when I have made such a proceeding safe."

"I wait anxiously," Gonzales sneered.

"The corporal and soldiers will retreat to that

far corner," Señor Zorro directed. "Landlord, you will accompany them. The Indian will go there too. Quickly, señores. Thank you. I do not wish to have any of you disturbing me while I am punishing this sergeant here."

"Ha!" Gonzales screeched in fury. "We shall soon see who does the punishing, my pretty fox!"

"I will hold the pistol in my left hand," Señor Zorro continued. "I will fight this sergeant with my right, in the proper manner. As I fight, I will keep an eye on the corner. The first move from any of you, señores, means that I fire. I am expert with this devil's weapon. If I fire, some men will cease to exist on this earth of ours. It is understood?"

The corporal and soldiers and landlord did not take the trouble to answer. Señor Zorro looked Gonzales straight in the eyes again, and a chuckle came from behind his mask.

"Sergeant, you will turn your back until I can draw my blade," he directed. "I give you my word as a caballero that I will not make an unfair attack."

"As a caballero?" Gonzales sneered.

"I said it, señor!" Zorro replied, his voice ringing a threat.

Gonzales shrugged his shoulders and turned his back. In an instant he heard the voice of the highwayman again.

"On guard, señor!"

CHAPTER 4

Swords Clash—
And Pedro Explains

Gonzales whirled at the word. He saw that Señor Zorro had drawn his sword, and that he was holding the pistol in his left hand high above his head. Moreover, Señor Zorro continued chuckling. The sergeant became infuriated. The blades clashed.

Sergeant Gonzales had been accustomed to battling with men who gave ground when they pleased and took it when they could, who went this way and that seeking an advantage, now advancing, now retreating, now swinging to left or right as their skill directed them.

But here he faced a man who fought in quite a different way. Señor Zorro seemed as if he were rooted to one spot. He did not give an inch, nor did he advance, nor step to either side.

Gonzales attacked furiously, as was his custom, and he found the point of his blade neatly turned aside. He used more caution then and tried what tricks he knew, but they gained him nothing. He attempted to pass around his opponent, and the other's blade drove him back. He tried a retreat, hoping to draw the other out, but Señor Zorro stood his ground and forced Gonzales to attack again. As for the highwayman, he did nothing except put up a defense.

Anger got the better of Gonzales then. He knew the corporal was jealous of him. The tale of this fight would be told to all the pueblo tomorrow, and so travel up and down the length of El Camino Real.

He attacked furiously, hoping to drive Señor Zorro off his feet and make an end of it. But he found that his attack ended as if against a stone wall. His blade was turned aside, his breast crashed against that of his foe. Señor Zorro merely threw out his chest and hurled him back half a dozen steps.

"Fight, señor!" Señor Zorro said.

"Fight yourself, cutthroat and thief!" the exasperated sergeant cried. "Don't stand like a stone, fool! Is it against your religion to take a step?"

"You cannot taunt me into doing so," the highwayman replied, chuckling again.

Sergeant Gonzales realized then that he had been angry. He knew an angry man cannot fight with the blade as well as a man who controls his temper. So he became deadly cold now. His eyes narrowed, and all boasting was gone from him.

He attacked again, but now he was alert,

looking for an unguarded spot. He fenced as he never had fenced in his life before. He cursed himself for having allowed wine and food to rob him of his wind. From the front, from either side, he attacked, only to be turned back again.

He had been watching his antagonist's eyes, of course, and now he saw a change. They had seemed to be laughing through the mask. But now they had narrowed and seemed to send forth darts of fire.

"We have had enough of playing," Señor Zorro said. "It is time for the punishment!"

And suddenly he began to press the fighting, taking step after step, slowly and methodically going forward and forcing Gonzales backward. The tip of his blade seemed to be a serpent's head with a thousand tongues. Gonzales felt himself at the other's mercy, but he gritted his teeth and tried to control himself and fought on.

Now he was with his back against the wall. He knew the highwayman was playing with him. He was ready to swallow his pride and call upon the corporal and soldiers to rush in and give him aid.

And then there came a sudden battering at the door, which the Indian had bolted. The heart of Gonzales gave a great leap. Somebody was there, wishing to enter. Whoever it was would think it peculiar that the door was not thrown open instantly by the fat landlord or his servant. Perhaps help was at hand.

"We are interrupted, señor," the highway-man said. "I regret it, for I will not have the time to give you the punishment you deserve. I will have to arrange to visit you another time, though you hardly are worth a double visit."

The pounding at the door was louder now. Gonzales raised his voice: "Ha! We have Señor Zorro here!"

"Coward!" the highwayman cried.

His blade seemed to take on new life. It darted in and out with a speed that was bewildering. It caught a thousand beams of light from the flickering candles and hurled them back.

And suddenly it darted in and hooked itself properly. Sergeant Gonzales felt his sword torn from his grasp and saw it go flying through the air.

"So!" Señor Zorro cried.

Gonzales awaited the stroke. A sob came into his throat that this must be the end instead of on a field of battle where a soldier wishes it. But no steel entered his breast to bring forth his life's blood. Instead, Señor Zorro swung his left hand down, passed the hilt of his blade to it and grasped it beside the pistol's butt. Then, with his right hand he slapped Pedro Gonzales once across the cheek.

"That for a man who mistreats Indians!" he cried.

Gonzales roared in rage and shame. Some-body was trying to smash the door in now. But

Señor Zorro appeared to give it little thought. He sprang back, and sent his blade into its scabbard like a flash. He swept the pistol before him, threatening all in the long room. He darted to a window, sprang onto a bench.

"Until a later time, señor!" he cried.

And then he went through the window as a mountain goat jumps from a cliff, taking its covering with him. In rushed the wind and rain, and the candles went out.

"After him!" Gonzales screeched, springing across the room and grasping his blade again. "Unbar the door! After him!"

The corporal reached the door first, and threw it open. In stumbled two men of the pueblo, eager for wine and an explanation of the fastened door. Sergeant Gonzales and his comrades drove over them, left them sprawling, and dashed into the storm.

But there was little use in it. It was so dark a man could not see a distance of a horse's length. The beating rain obliterated tracks almost instantly. Señor Zorro was gone—and no man could tell in what direction.

The shouting attracted the attention of the men of the pueblo. Sergeant Gonzales and the soldiers returned to the inn to find it full of men. And Sergeant Gonzales knew, also, that his reputation was now at stake.

"Nobody but a highwayman, nobody but a cutthroat and thief would have done it!" he cried aloud.

"How is that, brave one?" cried a man near the doorway.

"This pretty Señor Zorro knew, of course! Some days ago I broke the thumb of my sword hand while fencing at San Juan Capistrano. No doubt the word was passed to this Señor Zorro. And he visits me at such a time that he may afterward say he had vanquished me."

The corporal and soldiers and landlord stared at him, but none was brave enough to say a word.

"Those who were here can tell you, señores," Gonzales went on. "This Señor Zorro came in at the door and immediately drew a pistol—devil's weapon—from beneath his cloak. He points it at us, and forces all except me into that corner. I refused to go. 'Then you shall fight me,' says this pretty highwayman, and I draw my blade, thinking to make an end of the pest. And what does he tell me then? 'We shall fight,' he says 'In my left hand I hold the pistol. If your attack is not to my liking, I shall fire, and afterward run you through, and so make an end of a certain sergeant.'"

The corporal gasped. The fat landlord was almost ready to speak, but thought better of it when Sergeant Gonzales glared at him.

"Could anything be more devilish?" Gonzales asked. "I was to fight, and yet I would get a devil's chunk of lead in my carcass if I pressed the attack. Was there ever such a farce? It shows the stuff of which this pretty highwayman is made. Some day I will meet him when he holds no pistol—and then—"

"But how did he get away?" someone in the crowd asked.

"He heard those at the door. He threatened me with the pistol and forced me to toss my blade in the corner. He threatened us all, ran to the window, and sprang through. And how could we find him in the darkness or track him through the sheets of rain? But I am determined now! In the morning I go to Captain Ramón and ask permission to be freed from all other duty, that I may take some comrades and run down this pretty Señor Zorro. Ha! We shall go fox hunting!"

The excited crowd about the door suddenly parted, and Don Diego Vega hurried into the tavern.

"What is this I hear?" he asked. "They are saying that Señor Zorro has paid a visit here."

"It's true, caballero!" Gonzales answered. "If you hadn't gone home to work with your secretary, you would have seen the entire affair."

"You must tell me about it," Don Diego said. "But I pray you not make the tale too bloody. I cannot see why men must be violent. Where is the highwayman's dead body?"

Gonzales choked. The fat landlord turned away to hide his smile. The corporal and soldiers began picking up wine mugs to keep busy at this dangerous moment.

"He—that is, there is no body," Gonzales managed to say.

"Stop being modest, Sergeant!" Don Diego cried. "Am I not your friend? Did you not promise to tell me the story if you met this cutthroat? How much was the reward?"

"By the saints!" Gonzales swore.

"Come, Sergeant! Out with the tale! Landlord, give all of us wine, that we may celebrate this affair! Your tale, Sergeant! Will you leave the army, now that you have earned the reward? Will you purchase a hacienda and take a wife?"

Sergeant Gonzales choked again and reached gropingly for a wine mug.

"You promised me," Don Diego continued, "that you would tell me the whole thing, word by word. Did he not say so, landlord? You declared that you would relate how you played with him; how you laughed at him while you fought; how you pressed him back after a time and then ran him through—"

"By the saints!" Sergeant Gonzales roared, the words coming from between his lips like peals of thunder. "This is more than any man could endure! You—Don Diego—my friend—"

"Do not be so modest," Don Diego said. "You promised the tale, and I would have it. What does this Señor Zorro look like? Have you peered at the dead face beneath the mask? It is, perhaps, some man that we all know? Cannot some one of you tell me the facts? You stand here like so many speechless images of men—"

"Wine—or I choke!" Gonzales howled. "Don Diego, you are my good friend, and I will cross swords with any man who belittles you! But do not push me too far tonight—"

"I fail to understand," Don Diego said. "I have only asked you to tell me the story of the fight—how you mocked him as you battled; how you pressed him back at will, and then ended it by running him through—"

"Enough! Am I to be taunted?" the big sergeant cried. He gulped down the wine and hurled the mug to the floor.

"Is it possible that you did not win the battle?" Don Diego asked. "But surely this pretty highwayman could not stand up before you, my sergeant. What was the outcome?"

"He had a pistol—"

"Why did you not take it away from him, then, and push it down his throat? But perhaps that is what you did. Here is more wine, my sergeant. Drink!"

But Sergeant Gonzales was thrusting his way through the crowd at the door.

"I must not forget my duty!" he said. "I must hurry to the presidio and report this occurrence to the commandant!"

"But, Sergeant—"

"And as to this Señor Zorro, he will be meat for my blade before I am done!" Gonzales promised.

And then, cursing horribly, he rushed away through the rain. It was the first time in his life he ever had allowed duty to interfere with his pleasure and had run from good wine. Don Diego Vega smiled as he turned toward the fireplace.

CHAPTER 5

A Ride in the Morning

The following morning found the storm at an end. The sun was bright and palm fronds glistened in it. The air was refreshing as it blew down the valleys from the sea.

At midmorning, Don Diego Vega came from his house in the pueblo, drawing on his sheepskin riding gloves. His clothing was more gorgeous than usual this bright morning. Don Diego had dressed with much care,
spending a great deal of time over the polishing of his boots. He stood for a moment, glancing across the plaza at the little tavern. From the rear of the house an Indian servant led a horse.

Though Don Diego did not go galloping across the hills and up and down El Camino Real like an idiot, he owned a fine horse. The animal had spirit and speed and endurance. The elegant saddle showed more silver than leather on its surface. From the sides of the bridle dangled leather globes studded with semiprecious stones that glittered in the bright sunshine as if to advertise

31

Don Diego's wealth to all the world.

Don Diego mounted. A dozen or so men loitering around the plaza watched and made efforts to hide their grins. It was quite the thing in those days for a young man to spring from the ground into his saddle, gather up the reins, rake the beast's flanks with his great spurs, and disappear in a cloud of dust all in one motion.

But Don Diego mounted a horse as he did everything else—without haste or spirit. The servant held a stirrup, and Don Diego inserted the toe of his boot. Then he gathered the reins in one hand, and pulled himself into the saddle as if it were quite a task. Having done that much, the servant held the other stirrup and guided Don Diego's other boot into it. Don Diego clucked to the magnificent beast and started it, at a walk, along the edge of the plaza toward the trail that ran to the north.

Having reached the trail, Don Diego allowed the animal to trot, and after having covered a mile in this fashion, he urged the beast into a slow gallop, and so rode along the highway.

Men were busy in the fields and orchards and tending the herds. Now and then Don Diego passed a lumbering cart and saluted whoever happened to be in it. He traveled for a distance of four miles and then turned from the highroad into a narrow, dusty trail that led to a group of buildings against the side of a hill in the distance.

Don Diego Vega was about to pay a visit to the Hacienda of Don Carlos Pulido.

Don Carlos had experienced unexpected changes during the last few years. Once he had been second to none except Don Diego's father in position, wealth, and breeding. But he had made the mistake of getting on the wrong side of the fence politically. As a result, he found himself stripped of a part of his broad acres. And tax-gatherers sent by the governor had significantly reduced his former wealth. But, through it all, he had kept the dignity he was born with.

On this morning Don Carlos was sitting on the long covered porch of the hacienda. He sat alone on the veranda, thinking about how life had changed. His wife, Doña Catalina, the sweetheart of his youth and age, was inside directing her servants. His only child, the Señorita Lolita, was also inside, plucking at the strings of a guitar and dreaming as a girl of eighteen dreams. Don Carlos raised his silvered head and peered down the long, twisting trail. He saw in the distance a small cloud of dust. He feared that the single horseman who was approaching would be another gatherer of taxes. He shaded his eyes with a hand and watched the approaching rider carefully. He noted the leisurely manner in which he rode. Suddenly hope sang in his breast, for he saw the sun flashing from the silver on the saddle. He knew that tax gatherers did not have such rich harnesses.

The rider was now in plain sight from the veranda, and Don Carlos rubbed his eyes and looked again to confirm the suspicion he had. Even at that distance the aged don could recognize the horseman.

"It is Don Diego Vega," he breathed. "May the saints grant that my fortunes may now turn the better at last."

Don Diego, he knew, might only be stopping to pay a friendly visit. But even that would be something. The Vegas were a powerful family. If it became known that the Vega family was on excellent terms with the Pulido family, even the politicians would think twice before harassing Don Carlos further.

So Don Carlos clapped his hands together, and a servant hurried out from the house. Don Carlos ordered him to draw the shades to keep the sun from a corner of the veranda, and to place a table and some chairs, and to hurry with small cakes and wine.

He sent word into the house to the women, too, that Don Diego Vega was approaching. Doña Catalina felt her heart beginning to sing, and she herself began to hum a little song. Señorita Lolita ran to a window to look out at the trail. When Don Diego stopped before the steps that led to the veranda, there was a servant waiting to care for his horse. Don Carlos himself walked halfway down the steps and stood waiting, his hand held out in welcome.

"I am glad to see you as a visitor at my poor hacienda, Don Diego," he said, as the young man approached, drawing off his gloves.

"It is a long and dusty road," Don Diego said. "It tires me, too, to ride a horse the distance."

Don Carlos almost forgot himself and smiled at that, for surely riding a horse a distance of four miles was not enough to tire a young man of blood. But he remembered Don Diego's lifelessness and did not smile, for fear the smile would cause anger.

He led the way to the shady corner of the veranda, and offered Don Diego wine and cakes, and waited for his guest to speak. As was the custom, the women remained inside the house, not ready to show themselves unless they were called for.

"How are things in the pueblo of Reina de Los Angeles?" Don Carlos asked. "It has been almost a month since I visited there."

"Everything is the same," said Don Diego, "except that this Señor Zorro invaded the tavern last evening and had a duel with the big Sergeant Gonzales."

"Ha! Señor Zorro, eh? And what was the outcome of the fighting?"

"Though the sergeant has a crooked tongue while speaking of it," said Don Diego. "It has come to me through a corporal who was present that this Señor Zorro played with the sergeant and finally disarmed him and sprang through a window to make his escape in the rain. They could not find his tracks."

"A clever rascal," Don Carlos said. "At least, I have nothing to fear from him. It is generally known up and down El Camino Real, I suppose, that I have been stripped of almost everything the governor's men could carry away. I look for them to take the hacienda next."

"Um. Such a thing should be stopped!" Don Diego said, with more than his usual amount of spirit.

The eyes of Don Carlos brightened. If Don Diego Vega could be made to feel some sympathy, if one of the famous Vega family would but whisper a word in the governor's ear, the persecution would cease instantly. The commands of a Vega were obeyed by all men of whatever rank.

CHAPTER 6

Diego Seeks a Bride

Don Diego sipped his wine slowly and studied the twisting trail that led to the highway. Don Carlos looked at him in puzzled fashion. He realized that something was coming but scarcely knew what to expect.

"I did not ride through the sun and dust to talk with you about Señor Zorro, or any other bandit," Don Diego explained after a time.

"Whatever your errand, I am glad to welcome one of your family, caballero," Don Carlos said.

"I had a long talk with my father yesterday morning," Don Diego went on. "He reminded me that I am approaching the age of twenty-five. He feels that I am not accepting my responsibilities in the proper fashion."

"But surely—"

"Oh, doubtless he knows. My father is a wise man."

"And no man can dispute that, Don Diego."

"He urged upon me that I awaken and do as

I should. I have been dreaming, it appears. When my father dies I come into his fortune, naturally, being the only child. That part of it is all right. But what will happen when I die? That is what my father asks."

"I understand."

"A young man of my age, he told me, should have a wife and should—er—have offspring to inherit and preserve the family name."

"Nothing could be truer than that," said Don Carlos.

"So I have decided to get me a wife."

"Ha! It is something every man should do, Don Diego. Well do I remember when I courted Doña Catalina. We were mad to get into each other's arms, but her father kept her from me for a time. I was only seventeen, though, so perhaps he did right. But you are nearly twenty-five. Get a bride, by all means."

"And so I have come to see you about it," Don Diego said.

"To see me about it?" gasped Don Carlos, with something of fear and a great deal of hope in his heart.

"It will be rather a bore, I expect. Love and marriage, and all that sort of thing, is rather a necessary nuisance in its way. The idea of a man of sense chasing after a woman, playing a guitar for her, making up to her like a loon when everyone knows his intention! And then the ceremony! Being a man of wealth, I suppose the wedding must be an elaborate one."

"Most young men," Don Carlos observed, "delight to win a woman and are proud if they have a great and fashionable wedding."

"No doubt. But it is an awful nuisance. However, I will go through with it, señor. It is my father's wish, you see. You—if you will pardon me again—have fallen upon evil days. That is the result of politics, of course. But you are of excellent blood, señor, of the best blood in the land."

"I thank you for remembering that truth," said Don Carlos, rising long enough to put one hand over his heart and bow.

"Everybody knows it, señor. And a Vega, naturally, when he takes a mate, must seek out a woman of excellent blood."

"To be sure!" Don Carlos exclaimed.

"You have an only daughter, the Señorita Lolita."

"Ah! Yes, indeed, señor. Lolita is eighteen now, and a beautiful and accomplished girl, if her father may say it."

"I have observed her at the mission and at the pueblo," Don Diego said. "She is, indeed, beautiful, and I have heard that she is accomplished. Of her birth and breeding there can be no doubt. I think she would be a fit woman to preside over my household."

"Señor?"

"That is why I visit you today, señor."

"You—you are asking my permission to court to my fair daughter?"

"I am, señor."

Don Carlos's face beamed, and again he sprang from his chair, this time to bend forward and grasp Don Diego by the hand.

"She is a fair flower," the father said. "I would see her wed. I have been concerned about it, for I did not wish her to marry into a family that did not rank with mine. But there can be no question where a Vega is concerned. You have my permission, señor."

Don Carlos was delighted. A marriage between his daughter and Don Diego Vega! Such an alliance would restore his position. He would be important and powerful again!

He called a servant and sent for his wife. Within a few minutes the Doña Catalina appeared on the veranda to greet the visitor. Her face was beaming, for she had been listening.

"Don Diego has done us the honor to request permission to pay his respects to our daughter," Don Carlos explained.

"You have given consent?" Doña Catalina asked. It would be improper if she seemed too ready to jump for the man.

"I have given my consent," Don Carlos replied.

Doña Catalina held out her hand, and Don Diego gave it a loose grasp and then released it.

"Such an alliance would be a proud one," Doña Catalina said. "I hope that you may win her heart, señor."

"As to that," said Don Diego, "I trust there will be no undue nonsense. Either the lady wants me and will have me, or she will not. Will I change her mind if I play a guitar beneath her window, or hold her hand, or put my hand over my heart and sigh?"

"I—I—of course," said Don Carlos.

"Ah, señor, but a maid delights to be won," said the Doña Catalina. "It is her privilege, señor. The hours of courtship are held in memory during her lifetime. She remembers the pretty things her lover said, and the first kiss, when they stood beside the stream and looked into each other's eyes, and when he showed sudden fear for her while they were riding and her horse bolted— those things, señor. It is like a little game, and it has been played since the beginning of time. Foolish, señor? Perhaps when a person looks at it with cold reason. But delightful, nevertheless."

"I don't know anything about it," Don Diego protested. "I never ran around making love to women. You think it is necessary for me to do these things?"

"Oh," said Don Carlos, afraid of losing an influential son-in-law, "a little bit would not hurt.

A maid likes to be wooed, of course, even though she has made up her mind."

"I have a servant who plays the guitar wonderfully," Don Diego said. "Tonight I will order him to come out and play beneath the señorita's window."

"And not come yourself?" Doña Catalina gasped.

"Ride out here again tonight, when the chill wind blows in from the sea?" gasped Don Diego. "It would kill me. And the man plays the guitar better than I."

"I never heard of such a thing!" Doña Catalina gasped.

"Let Don Diego do as he wills," Don Carlos urged.

"I had thought," said Don Diego, "that you would arrange everything and then let me know. I would have my house put in order, of course, and get more servants. Is it not possible for you to attend to everything else? Just merely send me word when the wedding is to be."

Don Carlos Pulido was a little annoyed now.

"Caballero," he said, "when I courted Doña Catalina she kept me on needles and pins. One day she would frown, and the next day smile. It added a spice to the affair. I would not have had it different. You will regret it, señor, if you do not do your own courting. Would you like to see the señorita now?"

"I suppose I must," Don Diego said.

Doña Catalina went into the house to fetch the girl. Soon Señorita Lolita appeared, a dainty little thing with black eyes that snapped, and black hair that was wound around her head in a great coil, and dainty little feet that peeped from beneath skirts of bright color.

"I am happy to see you again, Don Diego," she said. He bowed and assisted her to one of the chairs.

"You are as beautiful as you were when I saw you last," he said.

"Always tell a señorita that she is *more* beautiful than when you saw her last," groaned Don Carlos. "Ah, that I were young again and could make love anew!"

He excused himself and entered the house. Doña Catalina moved to the other end of the veranda, so that the pair could talk privately, but from where she could watch, as a good duenna always must.

"Señorita," Don Diego said, "I have asked your father for permission to seek you in marriage."

"Oh, señor!" the girl gasped.

"Just say the word, señorita, and I shall tell my father, and your family will make arrangements for the ceremony. They can send word to me. It tires me to ride abroad when it is not at all necessary."

Now the pretty eyes of the Señorita Lolita began flashing a warning signal. But Don Diego, it was evident, did not see them, and so he rushed forward to his destruction.

"Will you agree to becoming my wife, señorita?" he asked, bending slightly toward her.

Señorita Lolita's face burned red, and she sprang from her chair, her tiny fists clenched at her side.

"Don Diego Vega," she replied, "you are of a noble family and have much wealth. But you are lifeless, señor! Is this your idea of courtship and romance? Can you not take the trouble to ride four miles on a smooth road to see the woman you would wed? What sort of blood is in your veins, señor?"

Doña Catalina heard that, and now she rushed across the veranda toward them, making signals to her daughter, which Señorita Lolita refused to see.

"The man who weds me must woo me and win my love," the girl went on. "He must touch my heart. Think you that I am some wench to give myself to the first man who asks? The man who becomes my husband must be a man with life enough in him to want me. Send your servant to play a guitar beneath my window? Oh, I heard, señor! Send him, señor, and I'll throw boiling water on him! *Buenos dias, señor!*"

She threw up her head proudly, lifted her

silken skirts aside, and swept into the house. Doña Catalina moaned once for her lost hopes. Don Diego Vega looked after the disappearing señorita and scratched at his head thoughtfully.

"I—I believe she is displeased with me," he said in his timid voice.

CHAPTER 7

A Different Sort of Man

Don Carlos lost no time in hurrying out to the veranda again. He had been listening and knew what had happened. He was anxious to smooth things over with the embarrassed Don Diego Vega. Though there was worry in his heart, he attempted to chuckle and make light of the occurrence.

"Women are fitful and filled with fancies, señor," he said. "At times they will speak sharply to those whom they in reality adore."

"But I—I hardly understand," Don Diego gasped. "I used my words with care. Surely I said nothing to insult or anger the señorita."

"She would be wooed, I take it, in the regular fashion. Do not despair, señor. Both her mother and I have agreed that you are a proper man for her husband. It is customary that a woman fight off a man to a certain extent, and then surrender. It appears to make surrender the sweeter. Perhaps the next time you visit us she will be more agreeable. I feel quite sure of it."

So Don Diego shook hands with Don Carlos Pulido and mounted his horse and rode slowly down the trail. Don Carlos turned about and entered his house again and faced his daughter, standing before her with his hands on his hips and looking at her with a sorrowful expression.

"He is the greatest catch in all the country!" Doña Catalina was wailing; and she dabbed at her eyes with a delicate square of filmy lace.

"He has wealth and position and could mend my broken fortunes if he were my son-in-law," Don Carlos declared, not taking his eyes from his daughter's face.

"He has a magnificent house and a hacienda besides, and the best horses in the area, and he is sole heir to his wealthy father," Doña Catalina said.

"One whisper from his lips into the ear of his excellency, the governor, and a man is made—or unmade," added Don Carlos.

"He is handsome—"

"I grant you that!" exclaimed the Señorita Lolita, lifting her pretty head and glaring at them. "That is what angers me! What a lover the man could be, if he would!"

"But he rode out here today to see you," Don Carlos said.

"Certainly it must have tired him!" the girl said. "Why does he let himself be made the laughingstock of the country? He is handsome and rich and talented. Yet he has scarcely enough energy to dress himself, I doubt not."

"This is all beyond me," the Doña Catalina wailed. "When I was a girl, there was nothing like this. An honorable man comes seeking you as his wife—"

"If he were less honorable and more of a man, I might look at him a second time," said the señorita.

"You must look at him more than a second time," put in Don Carlos, with some authority in his manner. "You cannot throw away such a fine chance. Think on it, my daughter. Be in a more friendly mood when Don Diego calls again."

Then he hurried to the patio on pretense that he wished to speak to a servant. But in reality he wanted to get away from the scene. Don Carlos knew better than to participate in an argument between his wife and his daughter.

Soon the siesta hour was at hand. Señorita Lolita went into the patio and settled herself on a little bench near the fountain. Her father was dozing on the veranda, and her mother in her room. The servants were scattered over the place, sleeping also. But Señorita Lolita could not sleep, for her mind was busy.

She knew her father's situation, of course, and she wanted, naturally, to see his fortunes improve again. She knew, too, that if she married Don Diego Vega, her father would regain his standing in the community. A Vega would not let the relatives of his wife be in any but the best of circumstances.

She called up a vision of Don Diego's handsome face, and wondered what it would be like if it were lighted with love and passion. It was a pity the man was so lifeless, she told herself.

The splashing of the water in the fountain lulled her to sleep, and she curled up at one end of the bench, her cheek pillowed on one tiny hand, her black hair cascading to the ground.

Suddenly she was awakened by a touch on her arm. She sat up quickly and would have screamed except that a hand was crushed against her lips to prevent her.

Before her stood a man whose body was enveloped in a long cloak, and whose face was covered with a black mask. She could see nothing of his features except his glittering eyes. She had heard Señor Zorro described, and she guessed that this was he. Her heart almost ceased to beat, she was so afraid.

"Silence, and no harm comes to you, señorita," the man whispered hoarsely.

"You—you are—" she questioned on her breath.

He stepped back, removed his sombrero, and bowed low before her.

"You have guessed it, my charming señorita," he said. "I am known as Señor Zorro, the

Curse of Capistrano."

"And—you are here—"

"I mean you no harm, no harm to any of this hacienda, señorita. I punish those who are unjust, and your father is not that. I admire him greatly. Rather would I punish those who do him evil than to touch him."

"I—I thank you, señor."

"I am weary, and the hacienda is an excellent place to rest," he said. "I knew it to be the siesta hour and thought everyone would be asleep. I am sorry to have awakened you, señorita, but I felt that I must speak. Your beauty would hinge a man's tongue in its middle so that both ends might be free to sing your praises."

Señorita Lolita had the grace to blush.

"If only my beauty affected other men so," she said.

"And does it not? Is it that the Señorita Lolita lacks suitors? That cannot be possible!"

"It is, nevertheless, señor. There are few bold enough to ally themselves with the family of Pulido, since it is out of favor. There is one—suitor," she went on. "But he does not seem to put much life into his wooing."

"Ha! A man lazy at love—and in your presence? What is wrong with the man? Is he ill?"

"He is so wealthy that I suppose he thinks he has but to ask and a maiden will agree to marry him."

"What an imbecile! It is the wooing gives the spice to romance."

"But you, señor! Somebody may come and see you here! You may be captured!"

"And do you not wish to see a highwayman captured? Perhaps it would mend your father's fortune if he were to capture me. The governor is not pleased with my activities."

"You—you had best go," she said.

"There speaks mercy in your heart. You know that capture would mean my death. Yet must I risk it, and stay a while."

He seated himself on the bench. Señorita Lolita moved away as far as she could, and then started to rise.

But Señor Zorro had been anticipating that. He grasped one of her hands and, before she guessed his intention, had bent forward, raised the bottom of his mask, and pressed his lips to its pink, moist palm.

"Señor!" she cried, and jerked her hand away.

"A man must express his feelings," he said. "I have not offended beyond forgiveness, I hope."

"Go, señor, or I call for help!"

"And get me executed?"

"You are but a thief! There is a reward offered for your capture."

"Such pretty hands would not handle blood money."

"Go!"

"Ah, señorita, you are cruel. A sight of you sends the blood pounding through a man's veins. A man would fight a horde at the bidding of your sweet lips."

"Señor!"

"A man would die in your defense, señorita. Such grace, such fresh beauty."

"For the last time, señor! I will cry out—and your fate be on your own head!"

"Your hand again—and I go."

"It may not be!"

"Then here I sit until they come and take me. No doubt I will not have to wait long. That big Sergeant Gonzales is on the trail, I understand, and may not be far away. He will have soldiers with him—"

"Señor, for the love of the saints—"

"Your hand."

She turned her back to him and held out her hand. Once more he pressed his lips to the palm. And then she felt herself being turned slowly, and her eyes looked deep into his. A thrill seemed to run through her. She realized that he still held her hand, and she pulled it away. And then she turned and ran quickly across the patio and into the house.

With her heart pounding at her ribs, she stood behind the curtains at a window and watched. Señor Zorro walked slowly to the fountain and stooped to drink. Then he put his sombrero on, looked once at the house, and stalked away. She heard the galloping hoofs of a horse die in the distance.

"A thief—yet a man!" she breathed. "If Don Diego had only half as much dash and courage!"

CHAPTER 8

Don Carlos Plays a Game

She turned away from the window, thankful that none of the household knew of Señor Zorro's visit. The remainder of the day she spent on the veranda, half the time working on some lace she was making, and the other half gazing down the dusty trail that ran toward the highway.

And then came evening. Inside the house the evening meal had been prepared, and the family was about to sit at table when someone knocked on the door.

A servant ran to open it, and Señor Zorro strode into the room. His sombrero came off, he bowed, and then he raised his head and looked at the speechless Doña Catalina and the half-terrified Don Carlos.

"I trust you will pardon this intrusion," he said. "I am the man known as Señor Zorro. But do not be frightened, for I have not come to rob."

Don Carlos got slowly upon his feet. Señorita Lolita gasped at this display of the man's courage, and feared he would mention the visit of the afternoon.

"Scoundrel!" Don Carlos roared. "You dare to enter an honest house?"

"I am no enemy of yours, Don Carlos," Señor Zorro replied. "In fact, I have done some things that should appeal to a man who has been persecuted."

That was true, Don Carlos knew, but he was too wise to admit it and so speak treason. He had no wish to offend the governor more by treating with courtesy this highwayman.

"What do you wish here?" he asked.

"I desire your hospitality, señor. In other words, I would eat and drink. I am a caballero, so my request is a reasonable one."

"Whatever good blood once flowed in your veins has been fouled by your actions," Don Carlos said. "A thief and highwayman has no right to the hospitality of this hacienda."

"I take it that you fear to feed me, since the governor may hear of it," Señor Zorro answered. "You may say that you were forced to do it. And that will be the truth."

Now one hand came from beneath the cloak, and it held a pistol. Doña Catalina shrieked and fainted, and Señorita Lolita cowered in her chair.

"You are doubly a scoundrel, since you frighten women!" Don Carlos exclaimed angrily. "Since it is death to refuse, you may have food. But I ask you to be caballero enough to allow me to remove my wife to another room and call a servant to care for her."

"By all means," Señor Zorro said. "But the señorita remains here as hostage for your good conduct and return."

Don Carlos glanced at the man, and then at the girl. He saw that his daughter was not afraid. He picked his wife up in his arms and carried her through the doorway, roaring for servants to come. Señor Zorro walked around the end of the table, bowed to Lolita again, and sat down in a chair beside her.

"This is foolhardiness, no doubt, but I had to see your beautiful face again," he said.

"Señor!"

"The sight of you this afternoon kindled a fire in my heart, señorita. The touch of your hand was new life to me."

Lolita turned away, her face flaming, and Señor Zorro moved his chair nearer and reached for her hand, but she eluded him.

"The longing to hear the music of your voice, señorita, may lure me here often," he said.

"Señor! You must never come again! I was lenient with you this afternoon, but I cannot be again. The next time I will call out, and you will be taken."

"You could not be so cruel," he said.

"Your fate would be on your own head, señor."

Don Carlos came back into the room. Señor Zorro arose and bowed once more.

"I trust your wife has recovered," he said. "I regret that the sight of my poor pistol frightened her."

"She has recovered," Don Carlos said. "I believe you said that you wished meat and drink. Now that I come to think of it, señor, you have indeed done some things that I have admired. I am happy to grant you hospitality for a time."

Don Carlos walked to the door, called a servant, and ordered that food and wine be brought. Don Carlos was well pleased with himself. Carrying his wife into the next room had given him his chance. One of the servants who had answered his call was particularly trustworthy. He had ordered the man to take the swiftest horse and ride like the wind the four miles to the pueblo, and there to spread the alarm that Señor Zorro was at the Pulido hacienda.

His object now was to delay Señor Zorro as much as possible. He knew the soldiers would come and the highwayman would be killed or captured. Surely the governor would admit that Don Carlos was entitled to some consideration for what he had done.

"You must have had some stirring adventures, señor," Don Carlos said as he returned to the table.

"A few," the highwayman admitted.

"There was that affair at Santa Barbara, for instance. I never did hear the details of that."

"I dislike speaking of my own work, señor."

"Please," the Señorita Lolita begged; and so Señor Zorro overcame his reluctance.

"It really was nothing," he said. "I arrived in the vicinity of Santa Barbara at sunset. There is a fellow there who runs a store, and he had been beating Indians and stealing from the friars. He would demand that the friars sell him goods from the mission, and then complain that the weight was short. The governor's men would make the friars deliver more. So I felt I must punish the man."

"Pray continue, señor," said Don Carlos, bending forward as if deeply interested.

"I dismounted at the door of his building and walked inside. He had candles burning, and there were half a dozen fellows trading with him. I covered them with my pistol and drove them into a corner and ordered this storekeeper before me. I frightened him thoroughly, and forced him to get the money he had in a secret hiding-place. And then I lashed him with a whip taken from his own wall, and told him why I had done it."

"Excellent!" Don Carlos cried.

"Then I sprang on my horse and dashed away. At an Indian's hut I made a sign, saying that I was a friend of the oppressed. Feeling particularly bold that evening, I galloped up to the door of the presidio, brushed aside the sentry—who took me for a courier—and pinned the sign to the door of the presidio with my knife. The soldiers came rushing out. I fired over their heads, and while they were bewildered I rode away toward the hills."

"And escaped!" Don Carlos exclaimed.

"I am here!—that is your answer."

"And why is the governor so particularly bitter against you, señor?" Don Carlos asked. "There are other highwaymen to whom he gives not a thought."

"Ha! I had a personal clash with his excellency. He was driving from San Francisco de Asis to Santa Barbara on official business, with an escort of soldiers about him. They stopped at a brook to refresh themselves, and the soldiers scattered while the governor spoke with his friends. I was hiding in the forest and dashed out at them. Instantly I was at the open door of the coach. I pointed my pistol at his head and ordered him to hand over his fat purse—which he did. Then I spurred through his soldiers, knocking several down as I went—"

"And escaped!" Don Carlos cried.

"I am here," said Señor Zorro.

The servant brought a tray of food and nervously placed it before the highwayman. He then left as quickly as possible.

"I am sure that you will pardon me," Señor

Zorro said, "when I ask you to sit at the far end of the room. As I take each bite, I must raise the bottom of my mask, for I have no wish to reveal my identity. I put the pistol before me on the table, so, to discourage treachery. I thank you, Don Carlos Pulido, for the meal you have so kindly furnished."

Don Carlos and his daughter sat where they had been directed. The bandit ate with evident pleasure. Now and then he stopped to talk to them, and once he had Don Carlos send out for more wine, declaring it to be the best he had tasted for a year.

Don Carlos was only too glad to oblige him. He was playing to gain time. He judged that his servant had reached the presidio at Reina de Los Angeles by now, and that the soldiers were on their way. If he could hold this Señor Zorro until they arrived!

"I am having some food prepared for you to carry with you, señor," he said. "You will pardon me while I get it? My daughter will entertain you."

Señor Zorro bowed, and Don Carlos hurried from the room. But Don Carlos had made a mistake in his eagerness. It was an unusual thing for a girl to be left alone in the company of a man, especially with a man known to be an outlaw. Señor Zorro guessed at once that he was being delayed purposely. It was an unusual thing for a man like Don Carlos to go for the food himself when there were servants that could be called. Don Carlos, in fact, had gone into the other room to listen at a window for sounds of galloping horses.

"Señor!" Lolita whispered across the room.

"What is it, señorita?"

"You must go—at once. I am afraid that my father has sent for the soldiers."

"And you are kind enough to warn me?"

"Do I wish to see you taken here? Do I wish to see fighting and bloodshed?" she asked.

"That is the only reason, señorita?"

"Will you not go, señor?"

"I hate to rush away from such a charming presence, señorita. May I come again at the next siesta hour?"

"By the saints—no! This must end, Señor Zorro. Go your way—and take care. You have done some things that I admire, so I would not see you captured. Go north to San Francisco de Asis and turn honest, señor. It is the better way. You must go now!"

"But could I depart without thanking your father for this meal?"

Don Carlos came back into the room then, and Señor Zorro knew by the expression on his face that the soldiers were coming up the trail. The don put a package on the table.

"Some food to carry with you, señor," he

said. "And we would enjoy more of your reminiscences before you start on your perilous journey."

"I have spoken too much of myself already, señor. It is not fitting for a caballero to do that. I must thank you and leave you now."

"At least, señor, drink another mug of wine."

"I fear," said Señor Zorro, "that the soldiers are much too close, Don Carlos."

The face of the don went white at that, for the highwayman was picking up his pistol. Don Carlos feared he was about to pay the price for his treacherous hospitality. But Señor Zorro made no move to fire.

"I forgive you this breach of hospitality, Don Carlos, because I am an outlaw and there has been a price put upon my head," he said. "I hold you no ill will because of it. *Buenos noches,* señorita! Señor, adios!"

Then a terrified servant who knew little concerning the events of the evening rushed in at the door. "Master! The soldiers are here!" he cried. "They are surrounding the house!"

CHAPTER 9

The Clash of Blades

On the table, near its middle, was a large candleholder in which a dozen of candles burned brightly. Señor Zorro sprang toward it. With one sweep of his hand he dashed it to the floor, extinguishing all the candles in an instant and plunging the room into darkness.

He evaded the wild rush of Don Carlos, springing across the room so lightly that his soft boots made not the slightest noise. For an instant Señorita Lolita felt a man's arm around her waist, gently squeezing it, felt a man's breath on her cheek, and heard a man's whisper in her ear:

"Until later, señorita."

Don Carlos was bellowing like a bull to direct the soldiers to the scene. Already some of them were pounding at the front door. Señor Zorro rushed from the room and into the kitchen. The servants fled before him as if he were a ghost, and he quickly extinguished all the candles that burned there.

Then he ran to the door that opened into the

patio. He raised his voice and gave a call that was half-moan and half-shriek, a peculiar call.

As the soldiers rushed in at the front door, and as Don Carlos called for the candles to be lighted, the sound of galloping hoofs was heard from the rear of the patio.

The sound of hoofs died away in the distance, but the soldiers had noted the direction in which the horse was traveling.

"The fiend escapes!" Sergeant Gonzales shrieked, he being in charge of the squad. "After him! I give the man who overtakes him one third of all the reward!"

The big sergeant rushed from the house, the men at his heels. They tumbled into their saddles and rode furiously through the darkness, following the sound of the beating hoofs.

"Lights! Lights!" Don Carlos was shrieking inside the house.

A servant came in and lighted the candles again. Don Carlos stood in the middle of the room, shaking his fists in helpless rage. Señorita Lolita crouched in a corner, her eyes wide with fear. Doña Catalina, fully recovered now from her fainting spell, came from her own room to see what the commotion was.

"The rascal got away!" Don Carlos said. "We can only hope the soldiers capture him."

"At least he is clever and brave," Señorita Lolita said.

"I grant him that, but he is a highwayman and a thief!" Don Carlos roared. "Why should he torment me by visiting my house?"

Señorita Lolita thought she knew, but she would be the last one to explain to her parents. There was a faint blush on her face yet because of the arm that had squeezed her and the words that had been whispered in her ear.

Don Carlos threw the front door open wide and stood in it, listening. To his ears came the sound of galloping hoofs once more.

"My sword!" he cried to a servant. "It is but one rider, by the saints! The rascal may be returning!"

The galloping stopped; a man made his way across the veranda and hurried through the door.

"Thank the good saints!" Don Carlos gasped.

It was not the highwayman. It was Captain Ramón, commandant of the presidio at Reina de Los Angeles.

"Where are my men?" the captain cried.

"Gone, señor! Gone after that pig of a highwayman!" Don Carlos informed him.

"He escaped?"

"He did, with your men surrounding the house. He dashed the candles to the floor, ran through the kitchen—"

"The men took after him?"

"They are on his heels, señor."

"Ha! Let us hope that they catch this pretty bird. He is a thorn in the side of the soldiery. This Señor Zorro is a clever gentleman, but he will be captured yet!"

And then Captain Ramón walked farther into the room and noticed the ladies. He swept off his cap and bowed before them.

"You must pardon my bold entrance," he said. "When an officer is on duty—"

"The pardon is granted freely," said Doña Catalina. "You have met my daughter?"

"I have not had the honor."

The doña introduced her, and Lolita retreated to her corner again and observed the soldier. He was not bad to look at—tall and straight and in a brilliant uniform.

The captain had been transferred from Santa Barbara to the post at Reina de Los Angeles only a month earlier. He had never set eyes upon Señorita Lolita before. But now that he had looked at her once, he looked a second time and a third. There was a sudden light in his eyes that pleased Doña Catalina. If Lolita could not look with favor upon Don Diego Vega, perhaps she would look with favor upon this Captain Ramón. To have her wedded to an officer would mean that the Pulido family would have some protection.

"I could not find my men now in the darkness," the captain said, "and so, if it is not presuming too much, I will remain here and await their return."

"By all means," Don Carlos said. "Be seated, señor, and I'll have a servant fetch wine."

"This Señor Zorro has about had his run," the captain said, after tasting the wine and declaring it excellent. "Now and then a man of his sort pops up and endures for a little day, but he never lasts long. In the end he meets his fate."

"That is true," said Don Carlos. "The fellow was boasting to us tonight of his accomplishments."

"I was commandant at Santa Barbara when he made his famous visit there," the captain explained. "I was visiting at one of the houses at the time or there might have been a different story. And tonight, when the alarm came, I was not at the presidio, but at the residence of a friend. That is why I did not ride out with the soldiers. As soon as I was notified, I came. It appears that this Señor Zorro has some knowledge of my whereabouts and is careful that I am not in a position to clash with him. I hope one day to do so."

"You think you could conquer him, señor?" Doña Catalina asked.

"Undoubtedly! I understand he really is an ordinary hand with a blade. He made a fool of my sergeant, but only because he held a pistol in one hand while he fenced. I would make short work of the fellow."

There was a closet in one corner of the room, and now its door opened a crack.

"The fellow should die the death," Captain Ramón went on to say. "He is brutal in his dealings with men. He kills for no reason, I have heard. They say he caused a reign of terror in the north, in the vicinity of San Francisco de Asis. He killed men, insulted women—"

The closet door was hurled open—and Señor Zorro stepped into the room.

"I shall take you to task for that statement, señor, since it is a falsehood!" the highwayman cried.

Don Carlos whirled around and gasped his surprise. Doña Catalina felt suddenly weak in the knees and collapsed on a chair. Señorita Lolita felt some pride in the man's statement, and a great deal of fear for him.

"I—I thought you had escaped," Don Carlos gasped.

"Ha! It was but a trick. My horse escaped—but I did not."

"Then there shall be no escape for you now!" Captain Ramón cried, drawing his blade.

"Back, señor!" Zorro cried, drawing a pistol. "I shall fight you gladly, but the fight must be fair. Don Carlos, gather your wife and daughter beneath your arms and go to the corner while I cross blades with this teller of falsehoods."

"I thought—you escaped!" Don Carlos gasped again, seemingly unable to think of anything else, and doing as Señor Zorro commanded.

"A trick!" the highwayman repeated, laughing. "It is a noble horse I have. Perhaps you heard a peculiar cry from my lips? My beast is trained to act at that cry. He gallops away wildly, making considerable noise, and the soldiers follow him. And when he has gone some distance he turns aside and stops, and after the pursuit has passed he returns to await my bidding. No doubt he is behind the patio now. I shall punish this captain and then ride away."

"With a pistol in your hand!" Ramón cried.

"I put the pistol upon the table—so. There it remains if Don Carlos stays in the corner with the ladies. Now, Captain!"

Señor Zorro extended his blade, and with a glad cry Captain Ramón crossed it with his own. Captain Ramón had some reputation as a master of fencing. Señor Zorro evidently knew it, for he was cautious at first, leaving no opening, on defense rather than attack.

The captain pressed him back, his blade flashing like streaks of lightning in a troubled sky. Now Señor Zorro was almost against the wall near the kitchen door, and in the captain's eyes the light of triumph already was beginning to burn. He fenced rapidly, giving the highwayman no rest, standing his ground and keeping his antagonist against the wall.

And then Señor Zorro chuckled. For now he understood the other's manner of combat, and knew that all would be well. The captain gave ground a little as the defense turned into an attack that puzzled him. Señor Zorro began laughing lightly.

"It would be a shame to kill you," he said. "You are an excellent officer, I have heard. But you have spoken falsehood regarding me, and so must pay a price. In a moment I shall run you through, but in such manner that your life will not emerge when I withdraw my blade."

"Boaster!" the captain snarled.

"As to that we shall see presently. Ha! I almost had you there, my captain. You are more clever than your big sergeant, but not half-clever enough. Where do you prefer to be touched— the left side or the right?"

"If you are so certain, run me through the right shoulder," the captain said.

"Guard it well, my captain, for I shall do as you say. Ha!"

The captain circled, trying to get the light of the candles in the highwayman's eyes, but Señor Zorro was too clever for that. He caused the captain to circle back, forced him to retreat, fought him to a corner.

"Now, my captain!" he cried.

And so he ran him through the right shoul-

der, as the captain had said, and twisted the blade a bit as he brought it out. He had struck a little low, and Captain Ramón dropped to the floor, a sudden weakness upon him.

Señor Zorro stepped back and sheathed his blade.

"I ask the pardon of the ladies for this scene," he said. "And I assure you that this time I am, indeed, going away. You will find that the captain is not badly injured, Don Carlos. He may return to his presidio within the day."

He removed his sombrero and bowed low before them, while Don Carlos sputtered and failed to think of anything to say. The masked man's eyes, for a moment, met those of the Señorita Lolita, and he was glad to find that in hers there was no dislike.

"*Buenos noches*," he said and laughed again.

CHAPTER 10

A Hint at Jealousy

Within the space of half an hour Captain Ramón's wounded shoulder had been cleansed and bandaged. The captain was sitting at one end of the table, sipping wine and looking very pale and tired.

Doña Catalina and Señorita Lolita had shown much sympathy. But the señorita could scarcely keep herself from smiling when she remembered the captain's boast about conquering the highwayman, and compared it to what had happened. Don Carlos was outdoing himself to make the captain feel at home—anything to avoid further offending the governor or one of his men. He had urged the officer to remain at the hacienda a few days until his wound had healed.

Having looked into the eyes of the Señorita Lolita, the captain had answered that he would be glad to remain at least for a day and was attempting polite and witty conversation, yet failing miserably. Once more there could be heard the drumming of a horse's hoofs, and Don Carlos sent a servant to the door. They supposed that it was one of the soldiers returning.

The horseman came nearer and then stopped before the house. The servant hurried out to care for the beast.

There were steps on the veranda, and Don Diego Vega hurried through the door.

"Ha!" he cried, as if in relief. "I am relieved that you all are alive and well!"

"Don Diego!" Don Carlos exclaimed. "You have ridden out from the pueblo a second time in one day?"

"No doubt I shall be ill because of it," Don Diego said. "Already my back aches. Yet I felt that I must come. There was an alarm in the pueblo, and it was said that this Señor Zorro had paid a visit to the hacienda. I saw the soldiers ride furiously in this direction, and fear came into my heart. You understand, Don Carlos, I feel—sure."

"I understand, caballero," Don Carlos replied, beaming upon him and glancing once at Señorita Lolita.

"I—er—felt it my duty to make the journey. And now I find that it has been made for nothing—you all are alive and well. How does it happen?"

Lolita sniffed, but Don Carlos was quick to make reply.

"The fellow was here, but he made his escape after running Captain Ramón through the shoulder."

"Ha!" Don Diego said, collapsing into a chair. "So you have felt his steel, eh, Captain? That should feed your desire for vengeance. Your soldiers are after the rogue?"

"They are," the captain replied shortly, for he did not like to have it said that he had been defeated in combat. "And they will continue to be after him until he is captured. I have a big sergeant, Gonzales—I think he is a friend of yours, Don Diego—who is eager to make the arrest and earn the governor's reward. I shall instruct him, when he returns, to take his squad and pursue this highwayman until he has been dealt with properly."

"Let us hope that the soldiers will be successful, señor. The scoundrel has annoyed Don Carlos and the ladies—and Don Carlos is my friend. I would have all men know it."

Don Carlos beamed, and Doña Catalina smiled bewitchingly, but the Señorita Lolita fought to keep her pretty upper lip from curling with scorn.

"A mug of your refreshing wine, Don Carlos," Don Diego Vega continued. "I am exhausted. Twice today have I ridden here from Reina de Los Angeles. It is about all a man can endure."

"It is not much of a journey—four miles," said the captain.

"Possibly not for a rough soldier," Don Diego replied, "but it is for a caballero."

"May not a soldier be a caballero?" Ramón asked, annoyed somewhat at the other's words.

"It has happened before now, but we come across it rarely," Don Diego said. He glanced at Lolita as he spoke, intending that she should take notice of his words, for he had seen the manner in which the captain glanced at her, and jealousy was beginning to burn in his heart.

"Do you mean to insinuate, señor, that I am not of good blood?" Captain Ramón asked.

"I cannot reply as to that, señor, having seen none of it. No doubt this Señor Zorro could tell me. He saw the color of it, I understand."

"By the saints!" Captain Ramón cried. "You dare to taunt me?"

"Never be taunted by the truth," Don Diego observed. "He ran you through the shoulder, eh? It is a mere scratch, I am sure. Should you not be at the presidio instructing your soldiers?"

"I await their return here," the captain replied. "Also, it is a tiring journey from here to the presidio, according to your own ideas, señor."

"But a soldier is used to hardship, señor."

"True, there are many pests he must encounter," the captain said, glancing at Don

Diego with meaning.

"You call me a pest, señor?"

"Did I say as much?"

This was perilous ground, and Don Carlos had no mind to let an officer of the army and Don Diego Vega have trouble in his hacienda. He feared it would cause him greater difficulties.

"More wine, señores!" he exclaimed in a loud voice, and stepping between their chairs in utter disregard of proper breeding. "Drink, my Captain, for your wound has made you weak. And you, Don Diego, after your wild ride—"

"I doubt its wildness," Captain Ramón observed.

Don Diego accepted the proffered wine mug and turned his back on the captain. He glanced across at Señorita Lolita and smiled. He got up deliberately and picked up his chair and carried it across the room to set it down beside her.

"And did the rogue frighten you, señorita?" he asked.

"Suppose he did, señor? Would you avenge the matter? Would you put blade at your side and ride until you found him, and then punish him as he deserves?"

"By the saints, were it necessary, I might do as much. But there are many men already chasing that rascal. Why should I risk my own neck?"

"Oh!" she exclaimed, exasperated.

"Let us not talk further of this bloodthirsty

Señor Zorro," he begged. "There are other things fit for conversation. Have you been thinking, señorita, on the question I asked earlier today?"

Señorita Lolita thought of it now. She remembered again what the marriage would mean to her parents and their fortunes. And she recalled the highwayman, too, and remembered his dash and spirit, and wished that Don Diego could be such a man. And she could not pledge herself to become Don Diego Vega's bride.

"I—I have scarcely had time to think of it, caballero," she replied.

"I trust you will make up your mind soon," he said.

"You are so eager?"

"My father was at me again this afternoon. He insists that I should take a wife as soon as possible. It is rather a nuisance, of course, but a man must please his father."

Lolita bit her lips because of her quick anger. Was a girl ever courted like this before? she wondered.

"I shall make up my mind as soon as possible, señor," she said finally.

"Will this Captain Ramón remain long at the hacienda?"

A little hope came into Lolita's breast. Was it possible that Don Diego Vega was jealous? If that were true, possibly there might be stuff in the man after all. Perhaps he would awaken, and love and passion come to him, and he would be as other young men.

"My father has asked him to remain until he is able to travel to the presidio," she replied.

"He is able to travel now. A mere scratch."

"You will not return tonight?" she asked.

"It probably will make me ill, but I must return. I must attend to some matters early in the morning. Business is such a nuisance."

"Perhaps my father will offer to send you in the carriage."

"Ha! It would be kind of him. A man may doze a bit in a carriage."

"But, if this highwayman should stop you?"

"I need not fear, señorita. Could I not purchase my release?"

"You would pay ransom rather than fight him, señor?"

"I have lots of money, but only one life, señorita. Would I be a wise man to risk having my blood let out?"

With this, Don Diego laughed lightly, as if it cost him an effort, and bent forward to speak in lower tones.

On the other side of the room, Don Carlos was doing his best to make Captain Ramón comfortable, and was glad that he and Don Diego remained apart for the time being.

"Don Carlos," the captain said, "I come

from a good family, and the governor is friendly toward me, as no doubt you have heard. I am only twenty-three years of age, otherwise I would hold a higher office. But my future is assured."

"I am glad to hear it, señor."

"I never set eyes upon your daughter until this evening, but she has captivated me, señor. Never have I seen such grace and beauty, such flashing eyes! I ask your permission, señor, to court the señorita."

CHAPTER 11

Three Suitors

Here was a problem for Don Carlos. He did not wish to anger Don Diego Vega or one of the governor's officers. How was he to get around this? If Lolita could not force her heart to accept Don Diego, perhaps she could learn to love Captain Ramón. After Don Diego, he was the best potential son-in-law in the area.

"Your answer, señor?" the captain asked.

"I trust you will not misunderstand me, señor," Don Carlos said, in lower tones. "I must make a simple explanation."

"Proceed, señor."

"Just this morning Don Diego Vega asked me the same question."

"Ha!"

"You know his blood and his family, señor. Could I refuse him? Of course not. But I may tell you this—the señorita weds no man unless it is her wish. So Don Diego has my permission to court my daughter, but if he fails to touch her heart—"

"Then I may try?" the captain asked.

"You have my permission, señor. Of course, Don Diego has great wealth, but you have a dashing way with you, and Don Diego—that is—he is rather—"

"I understand perfectly, señor," the captain said, laughing. "He is not exactly a brave and dashing caballero. Unless your daughter prefers wealth to a genuine man—"

"My daughter will follow the dictates of her heart, señor!" Don Carlos said proudly.

"Then the affair is between Don Diego Vega and myself?"

"So long as you use discretion, señor. I would have nothing happen that would cause difficulty between the Vega family and mine."

"Your interests shall be protected, Don Carlos," Captain Ramón declared.

As Don Diego talked, the Señorita Lolita observed her father and Captain Ramón, and guessed what was being said. It pleased her that a dashing officer was interested in her, and yet she had felt no thrill when first she looked into his eyes.

Señor Zorro, now, had thrilled her to the tips of her tiny toes. If Don Diego Vega were only more like the highwayman! If some man appeared who combined Vega's wealth with the rogue's spirit and dash and courage!

There was a sudden commotion outside, and into the room strode the soldiers, Sergeant

Gonzales at their head. They saluted their captain, and the big sergeant looked with wonder at his wounded shoulder.

"The rogue escaped us," Gonzales reported. "We followed him for a distance of three miles or so as he made his way into the hills, where we came upon him."

"Well?" Ramón questioned.

"He has allies."

"What is this?"

"Fully ten men were waiting for him there, my captain. They set upon us before we were aware of their presence. We fought them well, wounding three of them, but they made their escape. We had not been expecting a band, of course, and so rode into their ambush."

"Then we have to contend with a band of them!" Captain Ramón said. "Sergeant, you will select twenty men in the morning, and have command over them. You will take the trail of this Señor Zorro, and you will not stop until he is either captured or killed. I will add a quarter year's wages to the governor's reward, if you are successful."

"Ha! It is what I have wished!" Sergeant Gonzales cried. "Now we shall run this coyote to earth in short order! I will show you the color of his blood—"

"It would be just, since he has seen the color of the captain's," Don Diego put in.

"What is this, Don Diego, my friend? Captain, you have crossed blades with the rogue?"

"I have," the captain assented. "You but followed a tricky horse, my sergeant. The fellow was here, hiding in a closet. So it must have been some other man you met with his companions up in the hills. This Señor Zorro treated me much as he treated you in the tavern—had a pistol handy in case I should prove too expert with the blade."

Captain and sergeant looked at each other squarely, each wondering how much the other had been lying. Don Diego chuckled faintly and tried to press the Señorita Lolita's hand and failed.

"This thing can be settled only in blood!" Gonzales declared. "I will pursue the rascal until he is run to earth. With your permission, I will select my men in the morning."

"Sergeant Gonzales, I would like to go with you," Don Diego said suddenly.

"By the saints! It would kill you, caballero. Day and night in the saddle, uphill and downhill, through dust and heat, and with a chance at fighting."

"Well, perhaps it is best for me to remain in the pueblo," Don Diego admitted. "But he has annoyed this family, of which I am a true friend. At least you will keep me informed? You will tell me how he escapes if he dodges you? I at least may know that you are on his trail, and where you are riding, so I may be with you in spirit?"

"Certainly, caballero—certainly," Sergeant Gonzales replied. "Soon you will look upon the rogue's dead face. I swear it! My captain, do you return this night to the presidio?"

"Yes," Ramón replied. "Despite my wound, I can ride a horse."

He glanced toward Don Diego as he spoke, and there was almost a sneer upon his lips.

"What magnificent courage!" Don Diego said. "I, too, shall return to Reina de Los Angeles, if Don Carlos will be as good as to send for his carriage. I can tie my horse to the rear of it. To ride horseback the distance again this day would be the death of me."

Gonzales laughed and led the way from the house. Captain Ramón paid his respects to the ladies, scowled at Don Diego, and followed. The caballero faced Señorita Lolita again as her parents escorted the captain to the door.

"You will think about my question?" he asked. "My father will be at me again within a few days. I can avoid his anger if I am able to tell him that it is all settled. If you decide to marry me, have your father send me word by a servant."

"I will think about it," the girl said.

"Friar Felipe is at the mission of San Gabriel. He has been my friend from the time I was a boy, and I would have him say the words, unless you prefer otherwise. He could come to Reina de Los Angeles and read the ceremony in the little church on the plaza there."

"I will think about it," the girl said again.

"Perhaps I may come out again to see you in a few days, if I survive this night. *Buenos noches,* señorita. I suppose I should—er—kiss your hand?"

"You need not take the trouble," Señorita Lolita replied, "It might tire you."

"Ah—thank you. You are thoughtful, I see. I am fortunate if I get a thoughtful wife."

Don Diego sauntered to the door. Señorita Lolita rushed into her own room. She wrung her hands and tore at her hair a bit, too angry, too enraged to weep. Kiss her hand, indeed! Señor Zorro had not suggested it—he had done it. Señor Zorro had risked death to visit her. Señor Zorro had laughed as he fought, and then had escaped by a trick! Ah, if Don Diego Vega were half the man this highwayman seemed!

She heard the soldiers gallop away, and after a little time she heard Don Diego Vega depart in her father's carriage. And then she went out into the great room again to her parents.

"My father, it is impossible for me to marry Don Diego Vega," she said.

"What has caused your decision, my daughter?"

"I scarcely can tell, except that he is not the

sort of man I wish for my husband. He is lifeless; existence with him would be a continual torment."

"Captain Ramón also has asked permission to court you," Doña Catalina said.

"And he is almost as bad. I do not like the look in his eyes," the girl replied.

"You are too particular," Don Carlos told her. "If the persecution continues another year we shall be beggars. Here is the best catch in the country seeking you, and you would refuse him. And you do not like a high army officer because you do not fancy the look in his eyes. Think on it, girl! An alliance with Don Diego Vega is much to be desired. Perhaps when you know him better, you will like him more. And the man may awaken. I thought I saw a flash of it this night. He seemed jealous because of the presence of the captain here. If you can arouse his jealousy—"

Señorita Lolita burst into tears, but soon the tempest of weeping passed, and she dried her eyes.

"I—I shall do my best to like him," she said. "But I cannot bring myself to say, yet, that I will be his wife."

She hurried into her room again. Soon the house was in darkness. A gentle snore came from the room of Don Carlos Pulido and his wife.

But the Señorita Lolita did not slumber. She had her head propped on one hand, and she was looking through a window at the night sky, and her mind was full of thoughts of Señor Zorro. She remembered the grace of his bow, the music of his deep voice, the touch of his lips upon her palm.

"I wish he were not a rogue." She sighed. "How a woman could love such a man!"

CHAPTER 12

A Visit

Shortly after daybreak the following morning there was considerable commotion in the plaza at Reina de Los Angeles. Sergeant Pedro Gonzales was there with twenty troopers, almost all that were stationed at the local presidio. They were preparing for the chase of Señor Zorro.

The big sergeant's voice roared out above the noise as men adjusted saddles and inspected their water bottles and supplies. Sergeant Gonzales had ordered that his force travel light, and live off the country as much as possible. He had taken the orders of his captain seriously—he was going after Señor Zorro and did not propose to return until he had him—or had died trying to capture him.

"I will nail the fellow's hide to the presidio door, my friend," he told the fat landlord. "Then I will collect the governor's reward and pay the bill I owe you."

"I pray the saints it may be true," the landlord said.

"What, fool? That I pay you? Do you fear to lose a few small coins?"

"I meant that I pray you may be successful in capturing the man," the landlord said, telling the falsehood casually.

Captain Ramón was not up to see the start, having a small fever because of his wound. But the people of the pueblo crowded around Sergeant Gonzales and his men, asking questions. The sergeant found himself the center of interest.

"This Curse of Capistrano soon will cease to exist!" he boasted loudly. "Pedro Gonzales is on his trail. Ha! When I stand face to face with the fellow—"

The front door of Don Diego Vega's house opened at that moment, and Don Diego himself appeared. The townsmen wondered a bit at this, since it was so early in the morning. Sergeant Gonzales dropped a bundle he was handling, put his hands on his hips, and looked at his friend with sudden interest.

"Are you up so early?" he called. "Here is some devilish mystery that needs an explanation."

"You made noise enough to awaken the dead," Don Diego said.

"It could not be helped, caballero, since we are acting under orders."

"Was it not possible to make your preparations at the presidio instead of here in the plaza?

Or did you think not enough persons would see your importance there?"

"Now, by the—"

"Do not say it!" Don Diego commanded. "As a matter of fact, I am up early because I must make a miserable trip to my hacienda, a journey of some ten miles, to inspect the flocks and herds. Never become a wealthy man, Sergeant Gonzales, for wealth asks too much of a man."

"Something tells me that never shall I suffer on that account," said the sergeant, laughing. "If you should meet up with this Señor Zorro on your journey, he probably would hold you for a pretty ransom."

"Is he supposed to be between here and my hacienda?" Don Diego asked.

"Word arrived a short time ago that he had been seen on the road running to Pala and San Luis Rey. We ride in that direction. Since your hacienda is the other way, you will not meet the rascal now."

"I feel somewhat relieved to hear you say it. So you ride toward Pala, my sergeant?"

"We do. We will try to pick up his trail as soon as possible, and once we have it we will run this fox down. We start at once."

"I will await news eagerly," Don Diego said. "Good fortune go with you!"

Gonzales and his men mounted, and the sergeant shouted an order. They galloped across the plaza, raising great clouds of dust, and took the highway toward Pala and San Luis Rey.

Don Diego looked after them until nothing could be seen but a tiny dust cloud in the distance, then called for his own horse. He, too, mounted and rode away toward San Gabriel. Two servants rode mules and followed a short distance behind.

But before he departed, Don Diego wrote a message and had a servant carry it to the Pulido hacienda. It was addressed to Don Carlos, and read:

> The soldiers are starting this morning to pursue this Señor Zorro. It has been reported that the highwayman has a band of rogues under his command and may put up a fight. There is no telling, my friend, what may happen. I dislike the idea of your daughter, Doña Catalina, and you in the path of possible danger. What is more, this bandit saw your daughter last evening. He certainly must have appreciated her beauty and may seek to see her again.
>
> I beg of you to come at once to my house in Reina de Los Angeles, and make it as your home until matters are settled. I am leaving this morning for my hacienda, but have left orders with my servants that they are to do whatever you ask of them. I hope to see you when I return, which will be in two or three days.
>
> Diego.

Don Carlos read the letter aloud to his wife and daughter, and then looked up to see how they took it. He scoffed at the danger himself but did not wish to put his wife and daughter in jeopardy.

"What think you?" he asked.

"It has been some time since we have visited the pueblo," Doña Catalina said. "I have some friends left among the ladies there. I think it is an excellent thing to do."

"It certainly will not injure our fortunes to have it become known we are house guests of Don Diego Vega," Don Carlos said. "What does our daughter think?"

It was a concession to ask her, and Lolita realized that she was granted this unusual favor because of Don Diego's wooing. She hesitated some time before answering.

"I believe it will be all right," she said. "I should like to visit the pueblo, for we see scarcely anybody here at the hacienda. But people may talk concerning Don Diego and myself."

"Nonsense!" Don Carlos exploded. "Could there be anything more natural than that we should visit the Vegas, since our blood is almost as good as theirs?"

"But it is Don Diego's house, and not that of his father. Still—he will not be there for two or three days, he says, and we can return when he comes."

"Then it is settled," Don Carlos declared. "I will see my superintendent and give him instructions."

He hurried into the patio and rang the big bell for the superintendent. Don Carlos was well pleased for when the Señorita Lolita saw the rich furnishings in the house of Don Diego Vega, she might the more readily accept Don Diego as a husband, he thought.

Soon after the siesta hour, a cart was brought before the door, drawn by mules and driven by a servant. Doña Catalina and Lolita got into it, and Don Carlos mounted his best horse and rode at its side. And so they went down the trail to the highway, and down the highway toward Reina de Los Angeles.

They passed people who marveled to see the Pulido family traveling the road, for it was well known that they had met with ill fortune and rarely went anywhere now. But Doña Catalina and her daughter held their heads proudly, as did Don Carlos, and they greeted the people they knew, and so continued along the highway.

Soon they could see the pueblo in the distance—the plaza and the church with its high cross on one side of it and the inn and storehouses and a few fancy houses, like Don Diego's, and the scattered huts of Indians and poor folk.

The cart stopped before Don Diego's door. Servants rushed out to make the guests welcome, spreading a carpet from the cart to the doorway, so that the ladies would not have to step in the dust. Don Carlos led the way into the house, after ordering that the horse and mules be cared for. Once inside, they rested for a time, and the servants brought out wine and food.

They went through the rich house then, and even the eyes of Doña Catalina, who had seen many rich houses, widened at what she saw here in Don Diego's home.

"To think that our daughter can be mistress of all this when she speaks the word!" she gasped.

Señorita Lolita said nothing, but she began thinking that perhaps it would not be so bad after all to become the wife of Don Diego. She was fighting a mental battle. On the one side was wealth and position, and the safety and good fortune of her parents—and a lifeless man for husband; and on the other side was the romance and ideal love she craved. Until the last hope was gone she could not give the latter up.

Don Carlos left the house and crossed the plaza to the inn, where he met several older gentlemen. He renewed his acquaintance with them, but he noticed that none was enthusiastic in his greeting. They feared, he supposed, to appear openly friendly to him since he was in the bad graces of the governor.

"You are in the pueblo on business?" one asked.

"No, señor," Don Carlos replied. "This Señor Zorro is abroad, and the soldiers after him."

"We are aware of that."

"There may be a battle, or a series of raids, since it is whispered that Señor Zorro has a band of cutthroats with him. My hacienda is off by itself and would be at the mercy of the thief."

"Ah! And so you bring your family to the pueblo until the matter is at an end?"

"I had not thought of doing so, but this morning Don Diego Vega sent out to me a request that I bring my family here and make use of his house for the time being. Don Diego has gone to his hacienda, but will return within a short time."

The eyes of those who heard opened a bit at that. Don Carlos pretended not to notice, and went on sipping his wine.

"Don Diego was out to visit me yesterday morning," he continued. "We renewed old connections. And my hacienda had a visit from this Señor Zorro last night, as doubtless you have heard. Don Diego, learning of it, galloped out again, fearing we had met with disaster."

"Twice in one day!" gasped one of those who heard.

"I have said it, señor."

"You—that is—your daughter is very beautiful, is she not, Don Carlos Pulido? And seventeen, is she not—about?"

"Eighteen, señor. She is called beautiful, I believe," Don Carlos admitted.

Those around him glanced at one another. They had the solution now. Don Diego Vega was seeking to marry Señorita Lolita Pulido. That meant that Pulido's fortunes would soon return. He might well remember his friends and ignore those who had not stood by him. So now, they crowded forward, alert to do him honor. They asked concerning crops and the increase of his herds and flocks, and whether the bees were doing as well as usual, and did he think the olives were excellent this year.

Don Carlos appeared to take it all as a matter of course. He accepted the wine they bought, and bought them wine in return. The fat land-lord darted about serving them and trying to compute the day's profits in his head, which was a hopeless task for him.

When Don Carlos left the inn at dusk, several of them followed him to the door, and two of the more influential men walked with him across the plaza to the door of Don Diego's house. One of these begged that Don Carlos and his wife visit his house that evening for music and talk. Don Carlos graciously accepted the invitation.

Doña Catalina had been watching from a window, and her face was beaming when she met her husband at the door.

"Everything goes well," he said. "They have met me with open arms. And I have accepted an invitation for tonight."

"But Lolita?" Doña Catalina protested.

"She must remain here, of course. It will be all right. There are half a hundred servants around. Besides, I have accepted the invitation, my dear."

Such a chance to win favor again could not be disregarded, of course. Lolita was told of the arrangement. She was to remain in the great living room, reading a book of poetry she had found there. If she grew sleepy, she was to retire to a certain chamber. The servants would guard her, and the butler would look after her wishes personally.

Don Carlos and his wife went to make their evening visit. They were guided across the plaza by half a dozen servants carrying torches, for there was no moon, and rain was threatening again.

Señorita Lolita curled up on a couch, the book of poetry in her lap, and began to read. Each verse was about love, romance, passion. She marveled that Don Diego would read such a book, being so lifeless himself, but the volume showed that it had been much handled. She sprang from the couch to look at other books on a bench not far away. And her amazement increased.

Volume after volume of poets who sang of love; volumes that had to do with horsemanship; books by masters of the blade; tales of great generals and warriors were there.

Surely these books were not for a man of Don Diego's blood, she told herself. Don Diego was something of a puzzle, she told herself for the hundredth time; and she went back and began reading the poetry again.

Then Captain Ramón hammered at the front door.

CHAPTER 13

Love Comes Swiftly

The butler hurried to open it.

"I regret that Don Diego is not at home, señor," he said. "He has gone to his hacienda."

"I know as much. Don Carlos and wife and daughter are here, are they not?"

"Don Carlos and his wife are out on a visit this evening, señor."

"The señorita—"

"Is here, of course."

"In that case, I shall pay my respects to the señorita," Captain Ramón said.

"Señor! Pardon me, but the lady is alone."

"Am I not a proper man?" the captain demanded.

"It—it is scarcely right for her to receive the visit of a gentleman when her duenna is not present."

"Who are you to speak to me of what is proper?" Captain Ramón demanded. "Out of my way, scum! Cross me and you shall be punished. I know I can make trouble for you."

The face of the butler went white at that. The captain spoke the truth and, at a word, could cause him considerable trouble and perhaps a term in jail. Yet he knew what was right.

"But, señor—" he protested.

Captain Ramón thrust him aside with his left arm and stalked into the big living room. Lolita sprang up in alarm when she saw him standing before her.

"Ah, señorita, I trust that I did not startle you," he said. "I regret that your parents are absent, yet I must have a few words with you. This servant tried to prevent me from entering, but I imagine you have nothing to fear from a man with one wounded arm."

"It—it is scarcely proper, is it, señor?" the girl asked, a bit frightened.

"I feel sure no harm can come of it," he said.

He went across the room and sat down on one end of the couch and admired her beauty frankly. The butler hovered near.

"Go to your kitchen, fellow!" Captain Ramón snapped.

"No; let him stay," Lolita begged. "My father commanded it. He will be in trouble if he leaves."

"And if he remains. Go, fellow!"

The servant went.

Captain Ramón turned toward the girl again, and smiled. He flattered himself that he knew women—they loved to see a man show mastery over other men.

"More beautiful than ever, señorita," he said in a purring voice. "I am glad to find you alone, for there is something I wish to say to you."

"What is that, señor?"

"Last night at your father's hacienda I asked his permission to court you. Your beauty has inflamed my heart, señorita, and I would have you for my wife. Your father consented, except that he said Don Diego Vega also had received permission. So it appears that it lies between Don Diego and myself.

He paused for a moment.

"Certainly Don Diego Vega is not the man for you," he went on. "Has he courage, spirit? Is he not a laughingstock because of his weakness?"

"You speak ill of him in his own house?" the señorita asked, her eyes flashing.

"I speak the truth, señorita. I would have your favor. Can you not look upon me with kindness? Can you not give me hope that I may win your heart and hand?"

"Captain Ramón, this is not proper, and you know it," she said. "I beg you to leave me now."

"I await your answer, señorita."

Her outraged pride rose up at that. Why could she not be wooed as other señoritas, in the proper fashion? Why was this man so bold in his words? Why did he disregard the conventions?

"You must leave me," she said firmly. "This is all wrong, and you are aware of it. Would you destroy my name, Captain Ramón? Suppose somebody was to come and find us like this—alone?"

"Nobody will come, señorita. Can you not give me an answer?"

"No!" she cried, starting to get to her feet. "It is not right that you should ask it. My father, I assure you, shall hear of this visit!"

"Your father," he sneered. "A man who has the ill will of the governor. A man who is being destroyed because he possessed no political sense. I do not fear your father. He should be proud of the fact that Captain Ramón looks at his daughter."

"Señor!"

"Do not run away," he said, clutching her hand. "I have done you the honor to ask you to be my wife—"

"Done *me* the honor!" she cried angrily, and almost in tears. "It is the man who is honored when a woman accepts him."

"I like you when you rage," he observed. "Sit down again—beside me here. And now give me your answer."

"Señor!"

"You will marry me, of course. I will intercede with the governor for your father and get a part of his estate restored. I will take you to San

Francisco de Asis, to the governor's house, where you will be admired by persons of rank."

"Señor! Let me go!"

"My answer, señorita! You have held me off enough."

She wrenched away from him, confronted him with blazing eyes, her tiny hands clenched at her sides.

"Marry you?" she cried. "I would rather remain a maid all my life! I would rather die than marry you! I will marry a caballero, a gentleman, or no man! And I cannot say that you are such!"

"Pretty words from the daughter of a man who is about ruined."

"Ruin would not change the blood of the Pulidos, señor. I doubt whether you understand that, evidently having ill blood yourself. Don Diego will hear of this. He is my father's friend—"

"And you would wed the rich Don Diego, eh, and straighten out your father's affairs? You would not marry an honorable soldier, but would sell yourself—"

"Señor!" she shrieked.

This was beyond endurance. She was alone. There was nobody near to avenge the insult. So her blood called upon her to avenge it herself.

Like a flash of lightning her hand went forward and came against Captain Ramón's cheek with a crack. Then she sprang backward, but he grasped her by an arm and drew her toward him.

"I shall take a kiss to pay for that," he said. "Such a tiny bit of womanhood can be handled with one arm, thank the saints."

She fought him, striking and scratching at his breast, for she could not reach his face. But he only laughed at her and held her tighter until she was almost breathless. Then he threw back her head and looked down into her eyes.

"A kiss in payment, señorita," he said. "It will be a pleasure to tame such a wild one."

She tried to fight again, but could not. She called upon the saints to aid her. And Captain Ramón laughed more and bent his head, and his lips came close to hers.

But he never claimed the kiss. She started to wrench away from him again, and he was forced to strengthen his arm and pull her forward. And from a corner of the room there came a voice that was at once deep and stern.

"One moment, señor!" it said.

Captain Ramón released the girl and whirled on one heel. He blinked his eyes to pierce the gloom of the corner; he heard Señorita Lolita give a glad cry.

Then Captain Ramón, in spite of the presence of the lady, cursed, once and loudly, for Señor Zorro stood before him.

He did not pretend to know how the highwayman had entered the house; he did not stop to think of it. He realized that he was without a sword, and that he could not use it if he had one, because of his wounded shoulder. Señor Zorro was walking toward him from the corner.

"Outlaw I may be, but I respect women," the Curse of Capistrano said. "And you, an officer of the army, do not, it appears. What are you doing here, Captain Ramón?"

"What are *you* doing here?"

"I heard a lady's scream, which is reason enough for caballero to enter any place, señor. It appears to me that you have broken all the conventions."

"Perhaps the lady has broken them also."

"Señor!" roared the highwayman. "Another statement like that and I cut you down where you stand, though you are a wounded man! How shall I punish you?"

"Butler!" the captain shouted suddenly. "Here is Señor Zorro! A reward if you take him!"

The masked man laughed. "It will do you little good to call for help," he said. "Better to spend your breath in saying your prayers."

"You do well to threaten a wounded man."

"You deserve death, señor, but I suppose I must allow you to escape that. But you will go down upon your knees and apologize to this señorita. And then you will go from this house, slink from it like the dog you are, and keep your mouth closed regarding what has happened here. If you do not, I promise to soil my blade with your life's blood."

"Ha!"

"On your knees, señor, and instantly!" Señor Zorro commanded. "I am losing patience."

"I am an officer—"

"On your knees!" commanded Señor Zorro again, in a terrible voice. He sprang forward, grasped Captain Ramón by his well shoulder, and threw him to the floor.

"Quickly, coward! Tell the señorita that you humbly beg her pardon—which she will not grant, of course, since you are beneath speaking to. And swear to her that you will not annoy her again. Say it, or, by the saints, you have made your last speech!"

Captain Ramón said it. Then Señor Zorro grasped him by the neck, lifted him, propelled him to the door, and hurled him into the darkness.

Señor Zorro closed the door as the butler came running into the room, to stare in fright at the masked man.

"Señorita, I trust that I have been of service," the highwayman said. "That scoundrel will not bother you further, or he will feel the sting of my blade again."

"Oh, thank you, señor—thank you!" she cried. "I will tell my father this good deed you have done. Butler, get him wine!"

There was nothing for the butler to do

except obey, since she had commanded it. He hurried from the room, pondering on the times and the manners.

Señorita Lolita stepped to the man's side.

"Señor," she breathed, "you saved me from insult. You saved me from the pollution of that man's lips. Señor, though you think me too forward, I offer you freely the kiss he would have taken."

She put up her face and closed her eyes.

"And I will not look when you raise your mask," she said.

"It is too much, señorita," he said. "Your hand—but not your lips."

"You shame me, señor. I was bold to offer it, and you have refused."

"I would not have you feel shame," he said.

He bent swiftly, raised the bottom of his mask, and touched lightly her lips with his.

"Ah, señorita," he said. "I wish I were an honest man and could claim you openly. My heart is filled with love of you."

"And mine with love of you."

"This is madness. None must know."

"I would not be afraid to tell the world, señor."

"Your father and his fortunes! Don Diego!"

"I love you, señor."

"Your chance to be a great lady! Do you think I did not know Don Diego was the man

you meant when we spoke in your father's patio? This is a whim, señorita."

"It is love, señor, whether anything comes of it or not. And a Pulido does not love twice."

"What possibly could come of it but trouble?"

"We shall see. God is good."

"It is madness—"

"Sweet madness, señor."

He clasped her to him and bent his head again, and again she closed her eyes and took his kiss, only this time the kiss was longer. She made no effort to see his face.

"I may be ugly," he said.

"But I love you."

"Disfigured, señorita—"

"Still I love you."

"What hope can we have?"

"Go, señor, before my parents return. I will say nothing except that you saved me from insult and then went your way again. They will think that you came to rob Don Diego. And turn honest, señor, for my sake. Turn honest, I say, and claim me. No man knows your face, and if you take off your mask forever, none ever will know your guilt. It is not as if you were an ordinary thief. I know why you have stolen—to avenge the helpless, to punish cruel politicians, to aid the oppressed. I know that you have given what you have stolen to the poor. Oh, señor!"

"But my task is not yet done, señorita. I must finish it."

"Then finish it, and may the saints guard you, as I feel sure they will. And when it is finished, come back to me."

"I will not wait that long, señorita. I will see you often. I could not exist otherwise."

"Protect yourself."

"I will since now I have double reason. Life never was so sweet as now."

He backed away from her slowly. He turned and glanced toward a window.

"I must go," he said. "I cannot wait for the wine."

"That was only an excuse so that we could be alone," she confessed.

"Until the next time, señorita. May it not be long."

"Be careful, señor!"

"Always, loved one. Señorita, adios!"

Again their eyes met, and then he waved his hand at her, gathered his cloak close about his body, darted to the window, and went through it. The darkness outside swallowed him.

CHAPTER 14

Captain Ramón Writes a Letter

Picking himself up out of the dust before Don Diego Vega's door, Captain Ramón darted through the darkness to the footpath that ran up the slope toward the presidio.

His blood was aflame with rage, his face was purple with wrath. Only half a dozen soldiers remained at the presidio, the rest having gone with Sergeant Gonzales. Of these half-dozen, four were on the sick list and two were necessary as guards.

So Captain Ramón could not send men down to the Vega house in an effort to capture the highwayman. Besides, Captain Ramón did not wish to let it become known that this Señor Zorro had met him a second time. Could he give out the information that he had insulted a señorita and that Señor Zorro had punished him because of it? That Señor Zorro had caused him to get down upon his knees and apologize and then had kicked him through the front door like a dog?

The captain decided it was better to say nothing. He supposed that Señorita Lolita would tell her parents, and that the butler would give testimony. But he doubted whether Don Carlos would do anything about it. Don Carlos would think twice before challenging an officer of the army. Ramón only hoped that Don Diego would not learn of the event. If a Vega raised hand against him, the captain would have difficulty maintaining his position.

Pacing the floor of his office, Captain Ramón allowed his wrath to grow. He knew that the governor and his men were desperately in need of more funds to waste in riotous living. They had already plucked those men of wealth against whom there was the faintest breath of suspicion. They would welcome a new victim.

Maybe the captain could suggest one, and at the same time strengthen his own position with the governor? Would the captain dare hint that perhaps the Vega family was wavering in its loyalty to the governor?

At least he could do one thing, he decided. He could have his revenge for the scorn the señorita had shown him.

Captain Ramón grinned as the thought came to him. He called for writing materials and informed one of his well men that he should prepare for a journey to deliver a letter.

Ramón paced the floor for some minutes

more, thinking on the matter and trying to decide just how to word the letter he intended to write. Finally he sat down before the long table and addressed his message to his excellency the governor, at his mansion in San Francisco de Asis.

This is what he wrote:

I have received your orders that this highwayman, Señor Zorro, be stopped as soon as possible. I regret that I am unable at this time to report the rogue's capture.

I have the greater part of my force in pursuit of the fellow, with orders to get him in person or to bring me his corpse. But this Señor Zorro does not fight alone. He is being given protection at certain places in the neighborhood, allowed to remain in hiding when necessary, given food and drink and, no doubt, fresh horses.

Within the past day he visited the Hacienda of Don Carlos Pulido, a caballero known to be hostile to Your Excellency. I sent men there and went myself. While my soldiers took up his trail the man came from a closet in the living room at Don Carlos's house and attacked me treacherously. He wounded me in the right shoulder, but I fought him off until he became frightened and dashed away, making his escape. I may mention that I was hindered somewhat by this Don Carlos in pursuing the man. Also, when I arrived at the hacienda, it was obvious that the man had been eating his evening meal there.

The Pulido hacienda is an excellent place for such a man to hide, being somewhat off the main highway. I fear that Señor Zorro makes it his headquarters when he is in this vicinity. I await your instructions in the matter. I may add that Don Carlos scarcely treated me with respect while I was there, and that his daughter, the Señorita Lolita, scarcely could keep from showing her admiration of this highwayman and from sneering at the efforts of the soldiers to capture him.

There are also indications of a famous and wealthy family of this neighborhood wavering in loyalty to Your Excellency, but you will appreciate the fact that I cannot write of such a thing in a letter sent you by courier.

With deep respect,

Ramón, Commandant and Captain,

Presidio,

Reina de Los Angeles.

Ramón grinned again as he finished the letter. That last paragraph, he knew, would get the governor guessing. The Vega family was about the only famous and wealthy one that would fit the description. As for the Pulidos, Captain Ramón imagined what would happen to them. The governor would not hesitate to deal out punishment. Perhaps the Señorita Lolita would find herself without protection and in no position to reject the advances of a captain of the army.

Next Ramón wrote out a copy of the letter, intending to send one by his courier and keep the other for his files, in case something came up and he wished to refer to it.

Having finished the copy, he folded the original and sealed it, carried it to the soldiers' lounging room, and gave it to the man he had selected as courier. The soldier saluted and hurried out to his horse. He rode furiously toward the north, toward San Fernando and Santa Barbara, and on to San Francisco de Asis, with the orders ringing in his ears that he should make all haste.

Ramón returned to his office, poured out a measure of wine, and began reading over the copy of the letter. He half wished that he had made it stronger. Yet he knew that it was better to make it mild, for then the governor would not think he was exaggerating.

He stopped reading now and then to curse the name of Señor Zorro. And he frequently reflected on the beauty and grace of the Señorita Lolita and told himself she should be punished for the manner in which she had treated him.

He supposed that Señor Zorro was miles away by this time; but he was mistaken in that. For the Curse of Capistrano, as the soldiers called him, had not hurried away after leaving the house of Don Diego Vega.

CHAPTER 15

At the Presidio

Señor Zorro had gone a short distance through the darkness to where he had left his horse in the rear of a small hut. There he had stood, thinking of the love that had come to him.

After a few moments, he chuckled, then mounted and rode slowly toward the path that led to the presidio. He heard a horseman galloping away from the place and thought Captain Ramón had sent a man to call back Sergeant Gonzales and the troopers and put them on the fresher trail.

Señor Zorro knew how affairs stood at the presidio, knew to a man how many of the soldiers were there, and that four were ill with a fever, and that there was but one well man now besides the captain since one had ridden away.

He laughed again and made his horse climb the slope slowly so as to make little noise. In the rear of the presidio building he dismounted and allowed the reins to drag on the ground, knowing that the animal would not move from the spot.

He crept through the darkness to the wall of

the building and made his way around it carefully until he came to a window. He raised himself
on a pile of adobe bricks and peered inside.

He was looking into Captain Ramón's office.
He saw the commandant sitting before a table
reading a letter which, it appeared, he had just
finished writing. Captain Ramón was talking to
himself, as does many an evil man.

"That will cause trouble for the pretty señorita," he was saying. "That will teach her not to
scorn an officer of his excellency's forces. When
her father is in the jail charged with high treason,
and his estates have been taken away, then perhaps she will listen to what I have to say."

Señor Zorro had no difficulty in distinguish-
ing the words. Beneath his mask the face of Señor
Zorro grew black with rage.

He got down from the pile of adobe bricks
and slipped on along the wall until he came to
the corner of the building. At the side of the
front door a torch was burning. The only able-
bodied man left in the garrison was pacing back
and forth before the doorway, a pistol in his belt
and a blade at his side.

Señor Zorro noted the length of the man's
pacing. He judged the distance accurately, and
just as the man turned his back to resume his
march the highwayman sprang.

His hands closed around the soldier's throat
as his knees struck the man in the back. Instantly

they were on the ground, the surprised trooper doing his best to put up a fight. But Señor Zorro, knowing that a bit of noise might mean disaster for him, silenced the man by striking him on the temple with the heavy butt of his pistol.

He pulled the unconscious soldier back into the shadows, gagged him with a strip torn from the end of his serape, and bound his hands and feet with other strips. Then he drew his cloak about him, listened a moment to be sure he had not attracted the attention of any inside the building, and slipped once more toward the door.

He was inside in an instant. Before him was the big lounging room with its hard dirt floor. Here were some long tables and bunks and wine mugs and harnesses and saddles. Señor Zorro gave it a glance to assure himself that no one was there, and walked swiftly and almost silently across to the door that opened into the office of the commandant.

He threw the door open boldly. Captain Ramón was seated with his back toward it. He whirled around in his chair with a snarl on his lips, thinking one of his men had entered without knocking.

"Not a sound, señor," the highwayman warned, leveling his pistol at the captain's head. "You die if as much as a gasp escapes your lips."

He kept his eyes on those of the commandant,

closed the door behind him, and advanced into the room. He walked forward slowly. Captain Ramón had his hands on the table before him, and his face had gone white.

"This visit is necessary, señor, I believe," Señor Zorro said. "I have not made it because I admire the beauty of your face."

"What are you doing here?" the captain asked, speaking in a tone scarcely above a whisper.

"I happened to look in at the window, señor. I saw a letter before you on the table, and I heard you speak. It is a bad thing for a man to talk to himself. Had you remained silent I might have gone on about my business. As it is—"

"Well, señor?" the captain asked, with a bit of his old arrogance returning to him.

"I wish to read that letter before you."

"Does my military business interest you that much?"

"Kindly remove your hands from the table, but do not reach toward the pistol at your side unless you wish to die instantly. It would please me to have to send your soul into the hereafter."

The commandant did as he had been directed, and Señor Zorro went forward cautiously and snatched up the letter. Then he retreated a few paces again, still watching the man before him.

"I am going to read this," he said, "but I warn you that I shall watch you closely, also. Do not make a move, señor, unless it is your wish to visit your ancestors."

He read swiftly. When he had finished he looked the commandant straight in the eyes for some time without speaking, his own eyes glittering malevolently through his mask. Captain Ramón began to feel more uncomfortable.

Señor Zorro stepped across to the table, still watching the other. He held the letter to the flame of a candle. It caught fire, blazed, then dropped to the floor, a bit of ash.

"The letter will not be delivered," he said. "So you fight women, do you, señor? A brave officer and a credit to his excellency's forces! I am sure he would grant you promotion if he knew of this. You insult a señorita because her father is not friendly with those in power. And because she treats you as you deserve, you set about to cause trouble for the members of her family. Truly, it is a worthy deed."

He took a step closer and bent forward, still holding the pistol before him.

"Let me not hear of you sending any letter similar to the one I have just destroyed," he said. "I regret at the present time that you are unable to stand before me and cross blades. It would be an insult to my sword to run you through, but I would do it to rid the world of such a fellow."

"You speak bold words to a wounded man."

"No doubt the wound will heal, señor. And

when it has healed and you have back your strength, I will hunt you up and call you to account for what you have attempted to do this night. Let that be understood between us."

Again their eyes blazed, each man's into those of the other, and Señor Zorro stepped backward and drew his cloak closer about him. To their ears there came suddenly a jangling of harness, the tramp of horses' feet, the raucous voice of Sergeant Pedro Gonzales.

"Do not dismount!" the sergeant was crying to his men at the door. "I will only make report, and then we go on after the rogue! There will be no rest until we take him!"

Señor Zorro glanced quickly around the room, for he knew escape by the entrance was cut off now. Captain Ramón's eyes flashed with keen anticipation.

"Ho, Gonzales!" he shrieked before Zorro could warn him against it. "To the rescue, Gonzales! Señor Zorro is here!"

And then he looked at the highwayman defiantly, as if telling him to do his worst.

But Señor Zorro had no desire to fire his pistol and let out the captain's lifeblood, preferring to save him for the blade when his shoulder had healed.

"Remain where you are!" he commanded, and darted toward the nearest window.

The big sergeant had heard, however. He

called his men to follow, and rushed across the large room to the door of the office and threw it open. A bellow of rage escaped him as he saw the masked man standing beside the table, and saw the commandant sitting before it with his hands spread out before him.

"By the saints, we have him!" Gonzales cried. "In with you, troopers! Guard the doors! Some look to the windows!"

Señor Zorro had transferred his pistol to his left hand and had whipped out his blade. Now he swept it forward and sidewise, and the candles were struck from the table. Zorro put his foot on the only one that remained lighted and extinguished it—and the room was in darkness.

"Lights! Bring a torch!" Gonzales shrieked.

Señor Zorro sprang aside, against the wall, and made his way around it rapidly while Gonzales and two other men sprang into the room, and one remained guarding the door. In the other room several ran to get a torch, and managed to get in one another's way.

The man with the torch came rushing through the door finally, and he shrieked and went down with a sword blade through his breast. The torch fell to the floor and was extinguished. Before the sergeant could reach the spot, Señor Zorro was back in the darkness again and could not be found.

Gonzales was roaring his curses now and

searching for the man he wished to slay, and the captain was crying to him to be careful and not put his blade through a trooper by mistake. The other men were storming around. From the other room one came with a second torch.

Zorro's pistol spoke, and the torch was shot from the man's hand. The highwayman sprang forward and stamped on it, putting it out, and again retreated to the darkness, changing his position rapidly, listening for the deep breathing that would tell him the exact location of his various foes.

"Catch the rogue!" the commandant was shrieking. "Can one man make fools of the lot of you?"

Then he ceased to speak, for Señor Zorro had grasped him from behind and shut off his wind. Now the highwayman's voice rang out above the din.

"Soldiers, I have your captain! I am going to carry him before me and back out the door. I am going to cross the other room and so reach the outside of the building. I have discharged one pistol, but I am holding its mate at the base of the captain's brain. And when one of you attacks me, I fire, and you are without a captain."

The captain could feel cold steel at the back of his head, and he shrieked for the men to use caution. Señor Zorro carried him to the doorway and backed out with the captain held in front of him, while Gonzales and the troopers followed as closely as they dared, listening for every move, hoping for a chance to catch him off guard.

He crossed the big lounging room of the presidio and so came to the outside door. He was somewhat afraid of the men outside, for he knew that some of them had run around the building to guard the windows. The torch was still burning just outside the door, and Señor Zorro put up his hand and tore it down and extinguished it. But still there would be grave danger the moment he stepped out.

Gonzales and the troopers were before him, spread out fan-fashion across the room, bending forward, waiting for a chance to attack. Gonzales held a pistol in his hand and was watching for an opportunity to shoot without endangering the life of his captain.

"Back, señores!" the highwayman commanded now. "I would have more room in which to make my start. That is it—I thank you. Sergeant Gonzales, were not the odds so heavy, I might be tempted to fence with you and disarm you again."

"By the saints—"

"Some other time, my sergeant. And now, señores, attention! It hurts me to say it, but I had only the one pistol. What the captain has been feeling all this time at the base of his brain is nothing but a bridle buckle I picked up from the

CHAPTER 16

The Chase that Failed

Señor Zorro charged his horse down the treacherous slope of the hill, where there was loose gravel and a misstep would spell disaster, and where the troopers were slow to follow. Sergeant Gonzales possessed courage enough, and some of the men followed him. Others galloped off to right and left, planning to intercept the fugitive when he reached the bottom and turned.

Señor Zorro, however, was ahead of them, and took the trail toward San Gabriel at a furious gallop.

The troopers dashed along behind, calling to one another. Now and then they fired a pistol shot, but all missed their target.

Soon the moon came up. Señor Zorro had been anticipating that. He knew that it would make his escape more difficult. But his horse was fresh and strong, while those ridden by the troopers had covered many miles during the day, and so hope was not gone.

Now he could be seen plainly by his pursuers. He could hear Sergeant Gonzales crying for his men to ride faster. He glanced behind him as he rode and observed that the troopers were scattering out in a long line, the stronger and fresher horses pulling ahead of the others.

So they rode for some five miles, the troopers holding the distance, but not making any gain. Señor Zorro knew that soon their horses would weaken, and that his fine horse would outdistance them. Only one thing bothered him—he wanted to be traveling in the opposite direction.

Here the hills rose abruptly on either side of the highway, and it was not possible for him to turn aside and circle around the soldiers. If he attempted to have his horse climb, he would make slow progress, and the troopers would come within pistol range.

So he rode straight ahead, gaining a bit now. Two miles farther up the valley there was a trail that swung off to the right. By following it he would come to higher ground and so could double back on his tracks.

He had covered one of the two miles before he remembered that the higher trail had been blocked by a landslide caused by the recent torrential rain. He could not use it even when he reached it. And now a bold new thought came to his mind.

As he topped a slight rise in the terrain, he

glanced behind once more and saw that no two of the troopers were riding side by side. They were well scattered, and there was some distance between each two of them. It would help his plan.

He dashed around a bend in the highway and pulled up his horse. He turned the animal's head back in the direction he had come and bent forward in the saddle to listen. When he could hear the hoof beats of his nearest pursuer's horse, he drew his blade. Then he dug his spurs into his horse's flanks.

The animal he rode was not used to such treatment. The horse sprang forward like a thunderbolt, dashed around the curve like a wild stallion, and bore down on the nearest of Señor Zorro's foes.

"Make way," Señor Zorro cried.

The first man gave ground readily, not sure that this was the highwayman coming back. When he was sure of it, he shrieked the intelligence to those behind, but they could not understand because of the clatter of hoofs on the hard road.

Señor Zorro bore down on the second man, clashed swords with him, and rode on. He dashed around another curve, and his horse struck another powerfully, and hurled him from the roadway. Zorro swung at the fourth man, and missed him, and was glad that the soldier's counterstroke missed as well.

Now there was nothing but the straight ribbon of road before him, and his galloping foes dotting it. Like a maniac he rode them through, cutting and slashing at them as he passed. Sergeant Gonzales, far in the rear because of his exhausted horse, realized what was happening. He screeched at his men, and even as he screeched a thunderbolt seemed to strike his horse, throwing him to the ground.

And then Señor Zorro was through them and gone, and they were following him again, a cursing sergeant at their head, but at a distance slightly greater than before.

He allowed his horse to go somewhat slower now, since he could keep his distance. He rode to the first cross trail and turned into it. He reached higher ground and looked back to see the pursuit streaming out over the hill, losing itself in the distance, but still determined.

"It was an excellent trick," Señor Zorro said to his horse. "But we cannot try it often!"

He passed the hacienda of a man friendly to the governor, and a thought came to him— Gonzales might stop there and obtain fresh horses for himself and his men.

He was right. The troopers dashed up the driveway, and dogs howled a welcome. The master of the hacienda came to the door.

"We chase Señor Zorro!" Gonzales cried. "We require fresh steeds, in the name of the governor!"

The servants were called, and Gonzales and his men hurried to the corral. Magnificent horses were there, horses almost as good as the one the highwayman rode, and all were fresh. The troopers quickly stripped saddles and bridles from their exhausted mounts and put them on the fresh steeds. Then they dashed for the trail again and took up the pursuit. Señor Zorro had gained quite a lead, but there was only one trail he could follow, and they might overtake him.

Three miles away, on the crest of a small hill, there was a hacienda that had been presented to the mission of San Gabriel by a caballero who had died without leaving heirs. The governor had threatened to take it for the state but so far had not done so. The Franciscans of San Gabriel had protected their property with determination.

In charge of this hacienda was one Friar Felipe, a member of the order who was along in years. Under his direction the younger brothers of the order made the estate a profitable one, raising much livestock and sending to the storehouses great amounts of hides and tallow and honey and fruit, as well as wine.

Gonzales knew the trail they were following led to this hacienda, and that just beyond it there was another trail that split, one part going to San Gabriel and the other returning to Reina de Los Angeles by a longer route.

If Señor Zorro passed the hacienda, it was

likely that he would take the trail that ran toward the pueblo. If had he wished to go to San Gabriel, he would have continued along the highway in the first place, instead of turning and riding back through the troopers at some risk to himself.

But he doubted whether Zorro would pass. It was well known that the highwayman dealt harshly with those who prosecuted the friars, and it was probable that every Franciscan would give him aid.

The troopers came within sight of the hacienda and could see no light. Gonzales stopped them where the driveway started, and listened in vain for sounds of the man they pursued. He dismounted and inspected the dusty road, but could not tell whether a horseman had ridden toward the house recently.

He issued quick orders, and the troop separated, half of the men remaining with their sergeant and the others scattering in such manner that they could surround the house, search the huts of the Indians, and inspect the great barns.

Then Sergeant Gonzales rode straight up the driveway with half his men at his back, forced his horse up the steps to the veranda as a sign that he held this place in little respect, and knocked on the door with the hilt of his sword.

CHAPTER 17

Sergeant Gonzales Meets a Friend

In a short time, light showed through windows. A moment later the door was thrown open. Friar Felipe stood framed in it, shading a candle with his hand—a giant of a man now past sixty, but one who had been a power in his time.

"What is all this noise?" he demanded in his deep voice. "And why do you, son of evil, ride your horse on my veranda?"

"We are chasing this pretty Señor Zorro," Gonzales said.

"And you expect to find him in this poor house?"

"Stranger things have happened. Answer me, Friar! Have you heard a horseman gallop past recently?"

"I have not."

"And has this Señor Zorro paid you a visit recently?"

"I do not know the man."

"You have heard of him, doubtless?"

"I have heard that he aids the oppressed, that

he has punished those who have committed sacrilege, and that he has whipped those brutes who have beaten Indians."

"You are bold in your words, Friar."

"It is my nature to speak the truth, soldier."

"You will be getting yourself into difficulties with the powers, my robed Franciscan."

"I fear no politician, soldier."

"I do not like the tone of your words, Friar. I have half a mind to dismount and give you a taste of my whip!"

"Señor!" Friar Felipe cried. "Take ten years off my shoulders and I can drag you in the dirt!"

"That is a question for dispute. However, let us get to the subject of this visit. You have not seen a masked fiend who goes by the name of Señor Zorro?"

"I have not, soldier."

"I shall have my men search your house."

"You accuse me of falsehood?" Friar Felipe cried.

"My men must do something to pass the time, and they may as well search the house. You have nothing you wish to hide?"

"With your men as my guests, I had better hide the wine jugs," Friar Felipe said.

Sergeant Gonzales allowed an oath to escape him, and got down from his horse. The others dismounted, too, and the sergeant's horse was taken off the veranda.

Then Gonzales drew off his gloves, sheathed his sword, and stamped through the door with the others at his heels. Friar Felipe fell back before him, protesting against the intrusion.

From a couch in a far corner of the room arose a man. He stepped into the circle of light cast by the candleholder.

"As I have eyes, it is my raucous friend!" he cried.

"Don Diego! You here?" Gonzales gasped.

"I have been at my hacienda looking over business affairs. I rode over to spend the night with Friar Felipe, who has known me from baby-hood. These turbulent times! I thought that here, at least, I could rest in peace without hearing of violence and bloodshed. But it appears that I cannot. Is there no place in this country where a man may meditate and consult musicians and the poets?"

"Meal mush and goat's milk!" Gonzales cried. "Don Diego, you are my good friend and a true caballero. Tell me—have you seen this Señor Zorro tonight?"

"I have not, my sergeant."

"You did not hear him ride past the hacienda?"

"I did not. But a man could ride past and not be heard here in the house. Friar Felipe and I have been talking together. We were just about to retire when you came."

"Then the rogue has ridden on and taken the

trail toward the pueblo!" the sergeant declared.

"You had him in view?" Don Diego asked.

"Ha! We were upon his heels, caballero! But at a turn in the highroad he made connection with some twenty men of his band. They rode at us and attempted to scatter us, but we drove them aside and kept on after Señor Zorro. We managed to separate him from his fellows and give chase."

"You say he has twenty men?"

"At least twenty, as my men will testify. He is a thorn in the flesh of the soldiery, but I have sworn to get him! And when once we stand face to face—"

"You will tell me of it afterward?" Don Diego asked, rubbing his hands together. "You will relate how you mocked him as he fought, how you played with him, pressed him back, and ran him through—"

"By the saints! You make mock of me, caballero?"

"I am only joking, my sergeant. Now that we understand each other, perhaps Friar Felipe will give wine to you and your men. After such a chase, you must be fatigued."

"Wine would taste good," the sergeant said.

His corporal came in then to report that the huts and barns had been searched. No trace had been found of Señor Zorro or his horse.

Friar Felipe served the wine, though with

some reluctance. It was plain that he was doing it only because Don Diego had so requested.

"What will you do now, my sergeant?" Don Diego asked, after the wine had been brought. "Will you continue chasing around the country and creating an uproar?"

"The rogue evidently has turned back toward Reina de Los Angeles, caballero," the sergeant replied. "He thinks he is clever, no doubt, but I can understand his plan."

"Ha! And what is it?"

"He will ride around Reina de Los Angeles and take the trail to San Luis Rey. He will rest for a time, no doubt, to throw off all pursuit. Then he will continue to the vicinity of San Juan Capistrano. That is where he began this wild life of his, and for that reason he is called the Curse of Capistrano. Yes, he will go to Capistrano."

"And the soldiers?" Don Diego asked.

"We will follow him. We will work toward the place. When the news of his next outrage comes, we will be within a short distance of him instead of in the presidio at the pueblo. We can find the fresh trail and take up the chase. There will be no rest for us until the rogue is either slain or taken prisoner."

"And you have the reward," Don Diego added.

"That is true, caballero. The reward will come in handy. But I seek revenge, also. The rogue disarmed me once."

"Ah! That was the time he held a pistol in your face and forced you to fight not too well?"

"That was the time, my good friend. Oh, I have a score to settle with him."

"These turbulent times." Don Diego sighed. "I would they were at an end. A man has no chance for meditation. There are moments when I think I shall ride far out in the hills and spend some time there. Only in that manner may a man meditate."

"Why meditate?" Gonzales cried. "Why not cease thought and take to action? What a man you would make, caballero, if you let your eye flash now and then, and quarreled a bit, and showed your teeth once in a while. What you need is a few bitter enemies."

"May the saints preserve us!" Don Diego cried.

"It is the truth, caballero! Fight a bit—make love to some señorita—get drunk! Wake up and be a man!"

"Upon my soul! You almost persuade me, my sergeant. But—no. I never could endure the exertion."

Gonzales growled something into his great mustache and got up from the table.

"I have no special liking for you, Friar, but I thank you for the wine, which was excellent," he said. "We must continue our journey. A soldier's duty never is at an end."

"Do not speak of journeys!" Don Diego cried. "I must take one myself on the morrow. My business at the hacienda is done. I have to go back to the pueblo."

"I hope, my good friend, that you survive the hardship," Sergeant Gonzales said.

CHAPTER 18

Don Diego Returns

Señorita Lolita had to tell her parents, of course, what had happened during their absence. The butler would tell Don Diego when he returned, and the señorita was wise enough to realize that it would be better to make the first explanation.

The butler, having been sent for wine, knew nothing of what had happened between Señorita Lolita and Señor Zorro. She had told him merely that Señor Zorro had hurried away.

So the girl told her father and mother that Captain Ramón had called while they were absent, and that he had forced his way past the servant into the big living room to speak to her. Perhaps he had been drinking too much wine, or was not himself because of his wound, the girl explained. But he grew too bold and overstepped the bounds, finally insisting that he should have a kiss.

Whereupon, said the señorita, this Señor Zorro had stepped from the corner of the room—how he came to be there, she did not know—and had forced Captain Ramón to apologize, and then had thrown him out of the house. After which—and here she neglected to tell the entire truth—Señor Zorro made a courteous bow and hurried away.

Don Carlos was ready to go at once to the presidio and challenge Captain Ramón to mortal combat. But Doña Catalina was more calm. She convinced him that such action would announce to the world that their daughter had been affronted. Also, it would not aid their fortunes if Don Carlos quarreled with an officer of the army. In addition, the don was not a young man, and the captain probably would run him through in two passes and leave Doña Catalina a weeping widow, which she did not wish to be.

So the don paced the floor of the great living room and fumed and fussed and wished he were ten years the younger. He promised that when his daughter had married Don Diego, and he was once more in good standing, he would see that Captain Ramón was disgraced and his uniform torn from his shoulders.

Sitting in the bedroom that had been assigned to her, Señorita Lolita listened to her father's ravings, and found herself confronted with a problem. Of course, she could not marry Don Diego now. She had given her lips and her love to another, a man whose face she never had seen, a rogue pursued by soldiers—and she had spoken truly when she had said that a Pulido loved but once.

She was not prepared yet to tell her parents of the love that had come into her life. She dreaded the shock to them, and half feared that her father might send her away to some place where she never would see Señor Zorro again.

She crossed to a window and gazed out at the plaza—and she saw Don Diego approaching in the distance. He rode slowly, as if exhausted. His two servants rode a short distance behind him.

Men called to him as he neared the house, and he waved his hand at them lifelessly in response to their greeting. He dismounted slowly, one of the servants holding the stirrup and assisting him, brushed the dust from his clothes, and started toward the door.

Don Carlos and his wife greeted him, their faces beaming, for they had been accepted anew into society the evening before. They knew it was because they were Don Diego's houseguests.

"I regret that I was not here when you arrived," Don Diego said, "but I trust that you have been made comfortable in my poor house."

"More than comfortable in this gorgeous palace!" Don Carlos exclaimed.

"Then you have been fortunate. The saints know I have been uncomfortable enough."

"How is that, Don Diego?" Doña Catalina

asked.

"My work at the hacienda done, I rode as far as Friar Felipe's place, to spend a quiet night there. But as we were about to retire, there was a thundering noise at the door, and this Sergeant Gonzales and his soldiers entered. They had been chasing the highwayman called Señor Zorro, and had lost him in the darkness! The noisy fellows were with us an hour or more and then continued the chase. Because of them, I had a horrible nightmare and got very little rest. This morning I had to continue to Reina de Los Angeles."

"You have a difficult time," Don Carlos said. "Señor Zorro was here, caballero, in your house, before the soldiers chased him."

"Señor Zorro here?" Don Diego cried, sitting up straight in his chair with sudden interest.

"Undoubtedly he came to steal, or to kidnap you and hold you for ransom," Doña Catalina observed. "Don Carlos and I were visiting friends, and Señorita Lolita remained here alone. There—there is a distressing affair to report to you—"

"I beg you to proceed," Don Diego said.

"While we were gone, Captain Ramón called. He was told we were absent, but he forced his way into the house and made himself obnoxious to the señorita. This Señor Zorro came in and forced the captain to apologize and then drove him away."

"Well, that is what I call a pretty bandit!" Don Diego exclaimed. "The señorita suffers from the experience?"

"Indeed, no," said Doña Catalina. "She was of the opinion that Captain Ramón had taken too much wine. I will call her."

Doña Catalina went and called her daughter. Lolita came into the room and greeted Don Diego.

"It distresses me to know that you received an insult in my house," Don Diego said.

Doña Catalina made a motion to her husband, and they went to a far corner to sit, that the young folk might be somewhat alone. This seemed to please Don Diego, but not the señorita.

CHAPTER 19

Captain Ramón Apologizes

"Captain Ramón is a beast!" the girl said in a voice not too loud.

"He is a worthless fellow," Don Diego agreed.

"He—that is—he wished to kiss me," she said.

"And you did not let him, of course."

"Señor!"

"I—I did not mean that. Certainly you did not let him. I trust that you slapped his face."

"I did," said the señorita. "Then he struggled with me, and he told me that I should not be so particular, since I was daughter of a man who stood in the bad graces of the governor."

"Why, the horrible brute!" Don Diego exclaimed.

"Is that all you have to say about it, caballero? You do not understand, señor? This man came into *your* house, and insulted the girl you have asked to be *your* wife!"

"Confound the rascal! When next I see his excellency, I shall ask him to remove the officer to some other post."

"Oh!" the girl cried. "Have you no spirit at all? Have him removed? Were you a proper man, Don Diego, you would go to the presidio, you would call this Captain Ramón to account. You would pass your sword through his body to show that a man could not insult the señorita you admired and escape the consequences."

"It is such an exertion to fight," he said. "Let us not speak of violence. Perhaps I shall see the fellow and give him a talking to."

"Give him a talking to!" the girl cried.

"Let us discuss something else, señorita. Let us speak of the matter I mentioned the other day. My father will be after me again soon to know when I am going to take a wife. Cannot we get the matter settled in some manner? Have you decided on the day?"

"I have not said that I would marry you," she replied.

"Why hold off?" he questioned. "Have you looked at my house? I will do whatever you would like with it. You can refurnish it to suit your taste. You can have a new carriage."

"Is this your manner of wooing?" she asked, glancing at him from the corner of her eye.

"What a nuisance to woo," he said. "Must I play a guitar and make pretty speeches? Can you not give me your answer without all that foolishness?"

She was comparing this man with Señor

Zorro, and Don Diego did not compare to him favorably. She wanted to be done with this farce.

"I must speak frankly to you, caballero," she said. "I have searched my heart, and in it I find no love for you. I am sorry, for I know what our marriage would mean to my parents, and to myself in a financial way. But I cannot marry you, Don Diego, and it is useless for you to ask."

"Well, by the saints! I had thought it was about all settled," he said. "Do you hear that, Don Carlos? Your daughter says she cannot marry with me—that it is not in her heart to do so."

"Lolita, go to your room!" Doña Catalina exclaimed.

The girl did so gladly. Don Carlos and his wife hurried across the room and sat down beside Don Diego.

"I fear you do not understand women, my friend," Don Carlos said. "Never must you take a woman's answer for the last. She always may change her mind. A woman likes to keep a man off guard. Let her have her moods, my friend. In the end, I am sure, you shall have your way."

"It is beyond me!" Don Diego cried. "What should I do now? I told her I would give her all her heart desired."

"Her heart desires love, I suppose," Doña Catalina said.

"But certainly I will love and cherish her.

Does not a man promise that in the ceremony? Would a Vega break his word regarding such a thing?"

"Just a little courtship," Don Carlos urged.

"But it is such a nuisance."

"A few soft words, a pressure of the hand now and then, a sigh or two, a sad look from the eyes—"

"Nonsense!"

"It is what a maiden expects. Do not speak of marriage for some time. Let the idea grow on her—"

"But my father is liable to come to the pueblo any day and ask when I am to marry. He has practically ordered me to do it."

"No doubt your father will understand," said Don Carlos. "Tell him that her mother and myself are on your side and that you are winning the girl."

"I believe we should return to the hacienda tomorrow," Doña Catalina put in. "Lolita has seen this splendid house, and she will contrast it with ours. She will realize what it means to marry you. And there is an ancient saying that when a man and a woman are apart they grow fonder of each other."

"There is no need for you to hurry away."

"I think it would be best under the circumstances. Ride out to visit, say in three days. I am sure that you will find her more willing to listen."

"I presume you know best," Don Diego said. "But you must remain at least until tomorrow. I think I will go to the presidio and see this Captain Ramón. Possibly that will please the señorita. She appears to think I should call him to account."

Don Carlos was concerned that Don Diego knew so little about swords and fighting, but he said nothing. Even if a caballero went to his death, it was all right so long as he believed he was doing the proper thing and died as a caballero should.

So Don Diego went from the house and walked slowly up the hill toward the presidio building. Captain Ramón saw him approaching. He was surprised and snarled at the thought of fighting such a man.

But he was cold courtesy itself when Don Diego was ushered into the commandant's office.

"I am proud that you visit me here," he said, bowing low before the caballero.

Don Diego bowed in answer and took the chair Ramón indicated. The captain marveled that Don Diego had no sword with him.

"I was forced to climb this tiresome hill to speak to you on a certain matter," Don Diego said. "I have been informed that you visited my house during my absence and insulted a young lady who is my guest."

"Indeed?" the captain said.

"Were you deep in wine?"

"Señor?"

"That would excuse the offense in part. And, of course, you were wounded and probably had a fever. Did you have a fever, captain?"

"Undoubtedly," Ramón said.

"A fever is an awful thing. But you should not have intruded on the señorita. Not only did you offend her, but you offended me. I have asked the señorita to become my wife. The matter—er—is not settled as yet, but I have some rights in this case."

"I entered your house seeking news of this Señor Zorro," the captain lied.

"You—er—found him?" Don Diego asked. The face of the commandant flushed red.

"The fellow was there and he attacked me," he replied. "I was wounded, of course, and wore no weapon."

"It is most remarkable," observed Don Diego, "that none of you soldiers can meet this Curse of Capistrano when you can be on equal terms. Always he descends upon you when you are helpless, or threatens you with a pistol while he fights you with a blade, or has his twenty men about him. I met Sergeant Gonzales and his men at the Hacienda of Friar Felipe last night. The big sergeant told some distressing tale of the highwayman and his twenty men scattering his troopers."

"We shall get him yet," the captain promised. "And I might call your attention to certain significant things, caballero. Don Carlos Pulido, as we know, does not stand high with those in authority. This Señor Zorro was at the Pulido hacienda, you will remember, and attacked me there, emerging from a closet to do it."

"Ha! What do you mean?"

"Again, last night, he was in your house while you were away and the Pulidos were your guests. It begins to look as if Don Carlos has a hand in the work of the Señor Zorro. I am almost convinced that Don Carlos is a traitor. You had better think twice, before seeking to marry the daughter of such a man."

"By the saints, that is amazing!" Don Diego exclaimed, as if in admiration. "You really believe this?"

"I do, caballero."

"Well, the Pulidos are returning to their own place tomorrow. I only asked them to be my guests so they could be safe from this Señor Zorro's deeds."

"And Señor Zorro followed them to the pueblo. You see?"

"Can it be possible?" Don Diego gasped. "I must consider the matter. Oh, these turbulent times! But they are returning to their hacienda tomorrow. Of course I would not have his excellency think that I sheltered a traitor."

He got to his feet, bowed-courteously, and then stepped slowly toward the door. And there he seemed to remember something suddenly and turned to face the captain again.

"Ha! I almost forgot all about the insult!" he exclaimed. "What have you to say, my captain, regarding the events of last night?"

"Of course, caballero, I apologize to you most humbly," Captain Ramón replied.

"I suppose that I must accept your apology. But please do not let such a thing happen again. You frightened my butler badly, and he is an excellent servant."

Then Don Diego Vega bowed again and left the presidio. Captain Ramón laughed long and loudly, until the sick men in the hospital room feared that their commandant must have lost his wits.

"What a man!" the captain exclaimed. "I have turned him away from that Pulido señorita, I think. And I was a fool to hint to the governor that he could be capable of treason. I must correct that matter in some way. The man has not enough spirit to be a traitor!"

CHAPTER 20

Don Diego Shows Interest

The threatened rain did not come that day nor that night, and the following morning found the sun shining brightly and the sky blue and the scent of blossoms in the air.

Soon after the morning meal, the Pulido cart was driven to the front of the house by Don Diego's servants, and Don Carlos and his wife and daughter prepared to depart for their own hacienda.

"It upsets me," Don Diego said at the door, "that there can be no match between the señorita and myself. What will I say to my father?"

"Do not give up hope, caballero," Don Carlos advised him. "Perhaps when we are home again, and Lolita contrasts our humble house with your magnificence here, she will change her mind."

"I had thought all would be arranged before now," Don Diego said. "You think there is still hope?"

"I trust so," Don Carlos said. But he doubted

it, remembering the look that had been in the señorita's face. However, he intended having a serious talk with her once they were home.

The lumbering cart was driven away, and Don Diego Vega turned back into his house with his head hanging down, as it always hung when he took the trouble to think.

He decided that he needed companionship. He left the house to cross the plaza and enter the tavern. The fat landlord rushed to greet him, conducted him to a choice seat near a window, and fetched wine without being commanded to do so.

Don Diego spent the greater part of an hour looking through the window at the plaza, watching men and women come and go, observing the Indians, and now and then glancing up the trail that ran toward the San Gabriel road.

After a time, he observed two mounted men approaching down this trail. Between their horses walked a third man. Don Diego could see that ropes ran from this man's waist to the saddles of the horsemen.

"What, in the name of the saints, have we here?" he exclaimed, getting up from the bench and going closer to the window.

"Ha!" said the landlord at his shoulder. "That must be the prisoner coming now."

"Prisoner?" said Don Diego, looking at him. "Explain, fat one!"

"A friar is in trouble again. The man is to go before the magistrate immediately for his trial. They say that he swindled a dealer in hides, and now must pay the penalty."

"Who is the man?" Don Diego asked.

"He is called Friar Felipe, caballero."

"What is this? Friar Felipe is an old man, and my good friend. I spent night before the last with him at the hacienda he manages."

Don Diego showed some slight interest now. He walked briskly from the tavern and went to the office of the magistrate in a little adobe building on the opposite side of the plaza. The horsemen were just arriving with their prisoner. They were two soldiers who had been stationed at San Gabriel, the friars having been forced to give them bed and board in the governor's name.

It was Friar Felipe. He had been forced to walk the entire distance fastened to the saddles of his guards. There were indications that the horsemen had galloped now and then to test the friar's powers of endurance.

Friar Felipe's robe was almost in rags, and was covered with dust and perspiration. Those who crowded around him jeered and made fun of him. But the friar held his head proudly and pretended not to see or hear them.

The soldiers dismounted and forced him into the magistrate's office. The loiterers and Indians crowded forward and through the door. Don

Diego hesitated a moment, and then stepped toward the door.

He entered and pressed through the crowd. The magistrate saw him and beckoned him to a front seat. But Don Diego did not care to sit at that time.

"What is going on?" he demanded. "This is Friar Felipe, a godly man and my friend."

"He is a swindler," one of the soldiers retorted.

"If he is, then we can trust no man," Don Diego observed.

"The charges have been made, and the man is here to be tried," the magistrate insisted, stepping forward.

Then Don Diego sat down and court was convened. The man who made the complaint was an evil-looking fellow who explained that he was a dealer in hides and had a warehouse in San Gabriel.

"I went to the hacienda this friar manages and purchased ten hides," he testified. "After giving him the coins in payment and taking them to my storehouse, I found that the hides had not been cured properly. In fact they were ruined. I returned to the hacienda and told the friar as much, demanding that he return the money, which he refused to do."

"The hides were good," Friar Felipe put in. "I told him I would return the money when he returned the hides."

"They were spoiled," the dealer declared. "My assistant here will testify as much. They caused a stench, and I had them burned immediately."

The assistant testified as much.

"Have you anything to say, Friar?" the magistrate asked.

"It will do me no good," Friar Felipe said. "I already am found guilty and sentenced. Were I a follower of an immoral governor instead of a robed Franciscan, the hides would have been good."

"You speak treason?" the magistrate cried.

"I speak truth."

The magistrate puckered his lips and frowned. "There has been entirely too much of this swindling," he said finally. "Just because a man wears a robe does not mean he can rob at will. In this case, I find it proper to make an example, so friars will see they cannot take advantage of their calling. The friar must repay the man the price of the hides. And for the swindle he shall receive across his bare back ten lashes. And for the words of treason he has spoken, he shall receive five lashes additional. That is the sentence."

CHAPTER 21

The Whipping

The crowd jeered and applauded. Don Diego's face went white. For an instant his eyes met those of Friar Felipe. The caballero saw that the friar accepted the sentence as inevitable.

The office was cleared, and the soldiers led the friar to the place of execution in the middle of the plaza. Don Diego observed that the magistrate was grinning and he realized what a farce the trial had been.

"These turbulent times!" he said to a gentleman of his acquaintance who stood near.

They tore Felipe's robe from his back and started to lash him to the post. But the friar had been a man of great strength in his day, and some of it remained in his advanced years. He realized now what humiliation he was to suffer.

Suddenly he whirled the soldiers aside and stooped to grasp the whip from the ground.

"You have removed my robe!" he cried. "I am man now, not friar! One side, dogs!"

He lashed out with the whip. He cut a soldier

across the face. He struck at two Indians who sprang toward him. And then the crowd was on him, beating him down, kicking and striking at him, disregarding even the soldiers' orders.

Don Diego Vega felt moved to action. He could not see his friend treated in this manner. He rushed into the midst of the crowd. But he felt a hand grasp his arm and turned to look into the eyes of the magistrate.

"These are no actions for a caballero," the judge said in a low tone. "The man has been sentenced properly. When you raise hand to give him aid, you raise hand against his excellency. Have you stopped to think of that, Don Diego Vega?"

Don Diego had not. And he realized, too, that he could do no good to his friend by interfering now. He nodded his head to the magistrate and turned away.

But he did not go far. The soldiers had subdued Friar Felipe by now and had lashed him to the whipping post. The lash swung through the air, and Don Diego saw blood spurt from Friar Felipe's bare back.

He turned his face away then, for he could not bear to look. But he could count the lashes by the singing of the whip through the air. Proud old Friar Felipe was making not the slightest sound of pain.

He heard the crowd laughing and turned back again to find that the whipping was at an end.

"The money must be repaid within two days or you will have fifteen lashes more," the magistrate was saying.

Friar Felipe was untied and dropped to the ground at the foot of the post. The crowd began to melt away. Two friars who had followed from San Gabriel aided their brother to his feet and led him aside. Don Diego Vega returned to his house.

"Send me Bernardo," he ordered his butler.

Bernardo was a deaf servant for whom Don Diego had a peculiar use. Within the minute he entered the great living room and bowed before his master.

"Bernardo, you are a gem," Don Diego said: "You cannot speak or hear, cannot write or read. You are the one man in the world to whom I can speak without having my ears talked off in reply.

You do not 'Ha!' me at every turn."

Bernardo stood silently looking at Don Diego.

"These are turbulent times, Bernardo," Don Diego continued. "A man can find no place where he can meditate. Even at Friar Felipe's the night before last the big sergeant came pounding at the door. And this whipping of old Friar Felipe—Bernardo, let us hope that this Señor Zorro hears of the affair and acts accordingly."

Bernardo continued to look at the caballero.

"Bernardo, it is time for me to leave this pueblo for a few days. I will go to my father. I will tell him I have found no woman to marry me yet and ask his patience. And there, on the wide hills behind his house, I hope to find some spot where I may rest and consult the poets for one entire day without highwaymen and sergeants and unjust magistrates bothering me. And you, Bernardo, will accompany me, of course. I can talk to you without your taking the words out of my mouth."

Bernardo nodded. He guessed what was to come. It was a habit of Don Diego's to talk to him like this for a long time, and always there was a journey afterward.

Within a short time Don Diego set out, Bernardo riding mule a short distance behind him. They hurried along the highroad. Soon they caught up with a small cart, beside which walked two robed Franciscans, and in which was Friar Felipe, trying to keep back moans of pain. Don Diego dismounted beside the cart as it stopped. He went over to it and clasped Friar Felipe's hands in his own.

"My poor friend," he said.

"It is but another instance of injustice," Friar Felipe said. "For twenty years we of the missions have lived with it, and it grows. Our mistake was that we prospered. We did the work, and others reap the advantages."

Don Diego nodded, and the other went on:

"They began taking our mission lands from us, lands we had turned into gardens and orchards. They robbed us of worldly goods. And not content with that they now are persecuting us.

"The missions are doomed, caballero. The time is not far distant when mission roofs will fall in and the walls crumble away. Some day people will look at the ruins and wonder how such a thing could come to pass. But we can do nothing except submit. It is one of our principles. I did forget myself for a moment in the plaza at Reina de Los Angeles, when I took the whip and struck a man. It is our lot to submit."

"Sometimes," mused Don Diego, "I wish I were a man of action."

"You give sympathy, my friend, which is worth its weight in precious stones. And action expressed in a wrong channel is worse than no action at all. Where are you going?"

"To the hacienda of my father, good friend. I must ask his patience. He has ordered that I get me a wife, and I find it a difficult task."

"That should be an easy task for a Vega. Any maiden would be proud to take that name."

"I had hoped to marry the Señorita Lolita Pulido. But the señorita will have none of me," Don Diego complained. "It appears that I have not dash and spirit enough."

"She is hard to please, perhaps. Or possibly she is but playing hard to get with the hope of increasing your passion. A maid loves to tantalize a man, caballero. It is her privilege."

"I showed her my house in the pueblo and mentioned my great wealth and agreed to purchase a new carriage for her," Don Diego told him.

"Did you show her your heart, mention your love, and agree to be a perfect husband?"

Don Diego looked at him blankly, then blinked his eyes rapidly, and scratched at his chin, as he did sometimes when he was puzzled over a matter.

"What a perfectly silly idea!" he exclaimed after a time.

"Try it, caballero. It may have an excellent effect."

CHAPTER 22

Swift Punishment

As the cart drove off, Friar Felipe raised his hand in blessing. Don Diego Vega turned aside into the other trail, Bernardo following on the mule.

Back in the pueblo, the dealer in hides was the center of attention at the tavern. The fat landlord was busy supplying his guest with wine, for the dealer was spending a part of the money of which he had swindled Friar Felipe. The magistrate was spending the rest.

There was boisterous laughter as one recounted how the blood spurted from Friar Felipe's old back when the lash was applied.

"Not a whimper from him!" cried the dealer in hides. "He is a courageous old coyote! Now, last month we whipped one at San Fernando, and he howled for mercy. Someone said he had been ill and was weak, and maybe that was so. A tough lot, these friars. But it is great sport when we can make one howl. More wine, landlord! Friar Felipe is paying for it!"

There was a deal of laughter at that. The dealer's assistant, who had given perjured testimony, was tossed a coin and told to pretend to be a man and do his own buying. Whereupon the apprentice purchased wine for everyone, and howled merrily when the fat landlord gave him no change from his piece of money.

"Are you a friar, that you pinch coins?" the landlord asked.

Those in the tavern howled with merriment again, and the landlord, who had cheated the assistant to the limit, grinned as he went about his business. It was a great day for the fat landlord.

"Who was the caballero who showed some mercy toward the friar?" the dealer asked.

"That was Don Diego Vega," the landlord replied.

"He will get himself into trouble—"

"Not Don Diego," said the landlord. "You know the great Vega family, do you not, señor? If the Vegas held up as much as a little finger, there would be a political upheaval in these parts."

"Then he is a dangerous man?" the dealer asked.

A torrent of laughter answered him.

"Dangerous? Don Diego Vega?" the landlord cried, while tears ran down his fat cheeks. "You will be the death of me! Don Diego does nothing but sit in the sun and dream. He groans if he has to ride a few miles on a horse. Don

Diego is about as dangerous as a lizard basking in the sun. But he is an excellent gentleman, for all that!" the landlord added hastily, afraid that his words would reach Don Diego's ears, and Don Diego would take his business elsewhere.

It was almost dusk when the dealer in hides left the tavern with his assistant. Both staggered as they walked.

They made their way to the cart in which they traveled, waved their farewells to the group about the door of the tavern, and started slowly up the trail toward San Gabriel.

They made their journey in a leisurely manner, continuing to drink from a jug of wine they had purchased. They went over the crest of the first hill, and the pueblo of Reina de Los Angeles was lost to view. All they could see was the highway twisting before them like a great dusty serpent, and the brown hills.

Coming around a curve, they were confronted by a horseman. He was sitting easily in the saddle, with his horse standing across the road so that they could not pass.

"Turn your horse!" the dealer cried. "Do you want me to drive over you?"

The assistant gave an exclamation that was part of fear, and the dealer looked more closely at the horseman. His jaw dropped; his eyes bulged.

"By the saints! Señor *Zorro!*" he exclaimed. "Why would you bother me, Señor Zorro? I am a poor man, and have no money. Only yesterday, a friar swindled me, and I have been to the Reina de Los Angeles seeking justice."

"Did you get it?" Señor Zorro asked.

"The magistrate was kind, señor. He ordered the friar to repay me, but I do not know when I will get the money."

"Get out of the cart, and your assistant also!" Señor Zorro commanded.

"But I have no money—" the dealer protested.

"Out of the cart with you! Do I have to request it twice? Move before I shoot you!"

Now the dealer saw that the highwayman held a pistol in his hand. He squealed with fright and got out of the cart as speedily as possible, his assistant tumbling out at his heels. They stood in the dusty highway before Señor Zorro, trembling with fear.

"I have no money with me, kind highwayman, but I will get it for you!" the dealer begged. "I will deliver it whenever you wish—"

"Silence, beast!" Señor Zorro cried. "I do not want your money, perjurer. I know all about the farce of a trial at Reina de Los Angeles. I have ways of finding out about such things quickly. So the aged friar swindled you, eh? Liar and thief! It is you who are the swindler. And they gave that old and godly man fifteen lashes across his bare back because of the lies you told."

"I swear by the saints—"

"Do not. You have done enough false swearing already. Step forward."

The dealer did so, trembling. Señor Zorro dismounted swiftly and walked around in front of his horse. The dealer's assistant was standing beside the cart, his face white.

"Forward!" Señor Zorro commanded again.

Again the dealer did so. Suddenly he began to beg for mercy, for Señor Zorro had taken a mule whip from beneath his long cloak, and held it ready in his right hand, while he held the pistol in his left.

"Turn your back!" he commanded.

"Mercy, good highwayman! Am I to be beaten as well as robbed? You would whip an honest merchant because of a thieving friar?"

The first blow fell, and the dealer shrieked with pain. The second blow fell, and the dealer went to his knees in the dusty highroad.

Then Señor Zorro returned his pistol to his belt and stepped forward and grasped the dealer's mop of hair with his left hand, raising him up. With the right he rained heavy blows with the mule whip upon the man's back, until his tough coat and shirt were cut to ribbons and the blood soaked through.

"That for a man who perjures himself and has an honest friar punished!" Señor Zorro cried. And then he gave his attention to the assistant. "No doubt, young man, you but carried out your master's orders when you lied before the magistrate," he said. "But you must be taught to be honest and fair, no matter what the circumstances."

"Mercy, señor!" the assistant howled.

"Did you not laugh when the friar was being whipped? Are you not filled with wine now because you have been celebrating the punishment that godly man received for something he did not do?"

Señor Zorro grasped the youth by the nape of his neck, whirled him around, and sent a stiff blow at his shoulders. The boy shrieked and then began whimpering. Five lashes in all he received, for Señor Zorro apparently did not wish to render him unconscious. And finally he hurled the boy from him, and looped his whip.

"Let us hope both of you have learned your lesson," he said. "Get into the cart and drive on. And when you speak of this occurrence, tell the truth. If I hear otherwise, I will punish you again! Let me not learn that you have said some fifteen or twenty men surrounded and held you while I worked with the whip."

The apprentice sprang into the cart, and his master followed, and they disappeared in a cloud of dust toward San Gabriel. Señor Zorro looked after them for a time, then lifted his mask and wiped the perspiration from his face. Then he mounted his horse again, fastening the mule whip to the pommel of his saddle.

CHAPTER 23

More Punishment

Señor Zorro rode quickly to the crest of the hill. Beneath lay the pueblo. He stopped his horse and looked down at the village.

It was almost dark, but he could see well enough for his purpose. Candles had been lighted in the tavern. From the building came the sounds of loud song and drunken laughter.

Señor Zorro rode on down the hill. When he reached the edge of the plaza he put spurs to his horse and dashed up to the tavern. Half a dozen drunken men stood clustered near the door.

"Landlord!" he cried.

None of the men about the door gave any particular attention at first, thinking he was some caballero on a journey wishing refreshment. The landlord hurried out, rubbing his fat hands together, and stepped close to the horse. And then he saw that the rider was masked, and that the muzzle of a pistol was threatening him.

"Is the magistrate within?" Señor Zorro asked.

"*Si*, señor!"

"Stand where you are and pass the word for him. Say there is a caballero here who wishes speech with him regarding a certain matter."

The terrified landlord shrieked for the magistrate, and the word was passed inside. A moment later the judge came staggering out, crying in a loud voice to know who had summoned him from his pleasant entertainment.

He staggered up to the horse, put one hand against it, and looked up to find two glittering eyes regarding him through a mask. He opened his mouth to shriek, but Señor Zorro warned him in time.

"Not a sound or you die," he said. "I have come to punish you. Today you passed judgment on a godly man who was innocent. You knew he was innocent, and that his trial was a farce. By your order he received a certain number of lashes. You will have the same payment."

"You dare—"

"Silence!" the highwayman commanded. "You about the door there—come to my side!" he called.

They crowded forward, thinking that this caballero wished something done and had gold to pay for it. In the dusk they did not see the mask and pistol until they stood beside the horse, and it was too late to retreat then.

"We are going to punish this unjust magistrate," Señor Zorro told them. "The five of you will seize him now and conduct him to the post in the middle of the plaza, and there you will tie him. The first man to falter receives a slug of lead from my pistol. My sword will deal with the others. Now move!"

The frightened magistrate began to screech now.

"Laugh loudly, so that his cries will not be heard," the highwayman ordered. The men laughed as loudly as they could, although there was a peculiar quality to their laughter.

They seized the magistrate by the arms and conducted him to the post and bound him there with thongs.

"You will line up," Señor Zorro told them. "You will take this whip, and each of you will lash this man five times. I will be watching, and if I see the whip fall lightly once you will pay for it. Begin."

He tossed the whip to the first man, and the punishment began. Señor Zorro had no fault to find with the manner in which it was given, for there was great fear in the hearts of the men, and they whipped with strength, and willingly.

"You, also, landlord," Señor Zorro said.

"He will have me arrested for it afterward," the landlord wailed.

"Do you prefer jail or a coffin, señor?" the highwayman asked.

It became evident that the landlord preferred

the jail. He picked up the whip, and he surpassed the other men in the strength of his blows.

The magistrate was hanging heavily from the thongs now. Unconsciousness had come to him with about the fifteenth blow, more through fear than through pain.

"Unfasten the man," the highwayman ordered.

Two men sprang forward and did so.

"Carry him to his house," Señor Zorro went on. "And tell the people of the pueblo that this is how Señor Zorro punishes those who oppress the poor and helpless, who give unjust verdicts, and who steal in the name of the law. Go your ways."

The magistrate was carried away, groaning, consciousness returning to him now. Señor Zorro turned once more to the landlord.

"We shall return to the tavern," he said. "You will go inside and fetch me a mug of wine, and stand beside my horse while I drink it. It would be only a waste of breath for me to say what will happen to you if you attempt treachery on the way."

But the landlord's fear of the magistrate was as great as his fear of Señor Zorro. He went back to the tavern and hurried inside as if to get the wine. But he sounded the alarm.

"Señor Zorro is without," he hissed at those nearest the table. "He has just caused the magistrate to be whipped cruelly. He has sent me to get him a mug of wine."

Then he went on to the wine cask and began drawing the drink slowly as possible.

There was sudden activity inside the tavern. Some half-dozen caballeros were there, men who supported the governor. Now they drew their blades and began creeping toward the door. One of them held a pistol.

Señor Zorro, sitting his horse some twenty feet from the door of the tavern, suddenly saw the throng rush out at him, saw the light flash from half a dozen blades, heard the report of a pistol, and heard a ball whistle past his head.

The landlord was standing in the doorway, praying that the highwayman would be captured, for then he would be given some credit, and perhaps the magistrate would not punish him for having used the lash.

Señor Zorro reared his horse high in the air, and then raked the beast with the spurs. The animal sprang forward, into the midst of the caballeros, scattering them.

That was what Señor Zorro wanted. His blade already was out of its scabbard, and it passed through a man's sword arm, swung over and drew blood on another.

He fenced like a maniac, maneuvering his horse to keep his antagonists separated, so that only one could get at him at a time. Now the air was filled with shrieks and cries, and men came tumbling from the houses to see what was going on. Señor Zorro knew that some of them would have pistols, and while he feared no blade, he realized that a man could stand some distance away and cut him down with a pistol ball.

So he caused his horse to plunge forward again. Before the fat landlord realized it, Señor Zorro was beside him and had reached down and grasped him by the arm. The horse darted away, the fat landlord dragging, shrieking for rescue and begging for mercy in the same breath. Señor Zorro rode with him to the whipping post.

"Hand me that whip," he commanded.

The shrieking landlord obeyed, and called upon the saints to protect him. And then Señor Zorro turned him loose, and curled the whip around his fat middle. As the landlord tried to run, he cut at him again and again. He left him once to charge down on those who had blades and so scatter them, and then he was back with the landlord again, applying the whip.

"You tried treachery!" he cried. "Dog of a thief! You would send men about my ears, eh? I'll strip your tough hide—"

"Mercy!" the landlord shrieked, and fell to the ground.

Señor Zorro cut at him again, bringing forth a yell more than blood. He wheeled his horse and darted at the nearest of his foes. Another pistol ball whistled past his head, another man sprang at him with blade ready. Señor Zorro ran the man neatly through the shoulder and put spurs to his horse again. He galloped as far as the whipping post, and there he stopped his horse and faced them for an instant.

"There are not enough of you to make a fight interesting, señores!" he cried.

He swept off his sombrero and bowed to them in mockery. Then he wheeled his horse again and dashed away.

CHAPTER 24

At the Hacienda of
Don Alejandro

Behind him he left the town in an uproar. The shrieks of the fat landlord had aroused the pueblo. Men came running, servants hurrying at their sides and carrying torches. Women peered from the windows of the houses. Indians stood still wherever they happened to be and shivered, for it had been their experience that whenever there was an uproar, Indians paid the price.

Many young caballeros of hot blood were there. These young men crowded into the tavern and listened to the wails of the landlord. Some hurried to the house of the magistrate and saw his wounds and heard him rant about this insult to the law and his excellency the governor.

Captain Ramón came down from the presidio. When he heard the story, he swore great oaths. He sent his only well man to ride along the Pala Road to bring Sergeant Gonzales and his troopers back since they were following a false scent.

But the young caballeros saw a chance for excitement, and they asked permission of the commandant to form a posse and take after the highwayman, a permission they received immediately.

Some thirty of them mounted horses and set out. They intended to divide into three bands of ten each when they came to forks in the trail.

The townsmen cheered them as they started. They galloped rapidly up the hill and toward the San Gabriel road, making a deal of noise, glad that now there was a moon to let them see the foe when they approached him.

In time they separated, ten going toward San Gabriel proper, ten taking the trail that led to the Hacienda of Friar Felipe, and the last ten following a road that curved down the valley to a series of landed estates owned by wealthy dons.

Along this road, Don Diego Vega had ridden some time before, Bernardo behind him on the mule. Don Diego rode with leisure, and it was long after nightfall when he turned from the main road and followed a narrower one toward his father's house.

Don Alejandro Vega, the head of the family, sat alone at his table, the remains of the evening meal before him, when he heard a horseman before the door. A servant ran to open it, and Don Diego entered, Bernardo following close behind him.

"Ah, Diego, my son!" the old don cried, extending his arms.

Don Diego was clasped for an instant to his father's breast, and then he sat down beside the table and took a mug of wine. Having refreshed himself, he faced Don Alejandro once more.

"It has been a tiring journey," he remarked.

"And what is the cause of your journey, my son?"

"I felt that I should come to the hacienda," Don Diego said. "It is no time to be in the pueblo. Wherever a man turns, he finds nothing but violence and bloodshed. This Señor Zorro—"

"Ha! What of him?"

"Please do not 'Ha!' me, sir and father. I have been 'Ha'd!' at from morning until night the past several days. These are turbulent times. This Señor Zorro has made a visit to the Pulido hacienda and frightened everyone there. I went to my hacienda on business, and from there I went over to see old Friar Felipe, thinking I might get a chance to meditate in his presence. And who makes an appearance but a big sergeant and his troopers seeking this Señor Zorro."

"They caught him?"

"I believe not, father. I returned to the pueblo; and what think you happened there today? They brought in Friar Felipe, accused of having swindled a dealer, and after mockery of a trial they lashed him to a post and gave him the whip fifteen times across his back."

"The scoundrels!" Don Alejandro cried.

"I could no longer stand it, and so I decided to pay you a visit. Wherever I turn there is turmoil. It is enough to make a man insane."

"You have something else to tell me?" Don Alejandro asked his son, looking at him searchingly.

"By the saints! I had hoped to avoid it, father."

"Let me hear about it."

"I paid a visit to the Pulido hacienda and spoke with Don Carlos and his wife, also the Señorita Lolita."

"You were pleased with the señorita?"

"She is as lovely as any girl I have met," Don Diego said. "I spoke to Don Carlos of the matter of marriage, and he appeared to be delighted."

"Ah! He would be," said Don Alejandro.

"But the marriage cannot take place, I fear. She will have none of me."

"How is this? Refuses to wed with a Vega? Refuses to become allied to the most powerful family in the country, with the best blood in the land?"

"She suggested, father, that I am not the sort of man for her. She would have me play a guitar under her window, perhaps, and make eyes, and hold hands when her duenna is not looking, and all that silliness."

"By the saints! Are you a Vega?" Don Alejandro cried. "Would not any worthy man want a chance like that? Would not any caballero delight to serenade his love on a moonlit night? The little things you term silly are the very essence of love. I am not surprised the señorita was displeased with you."

"I did not see that such things were necessary," Don Diego said.

"Did you go to the señorita in a cold-blooded manner and suggest that you marry and be done with it? Did you think, young sir, that you were purchasing a horse or a bull? By the saints! And so there is no chance for you to marry the girl? She has the best blood by far, next to our own."

"Don Carlos told me to have hope," Diego replied. "He took her back to the hacienda, and suggested that perhaps when she had been there a time she might change her mind."

"She is yours, if you play the game," Don Alejandro said. "You are a Vega, and therefore the best catch in the country. Be but half a lover, and the señorita is yours. What sort of blood is in your veins? I have half a mind to slit one of them and see."

"Could we put this marriage business aside for the time being?" Don Diego asked.

"You are twenty-five. I was quite old when you were born. Soon I shall go the way of my fathers. You are the only son, the heir, and you must have a wife and offspring. Is the Vega family to die out because your blood is water? Win you a wife within the quarter-year, young sir, and a wife I can accept into the family, or I leave my wealth to the Franciscans when I pass away."

"My father!"

"I mean it. Get life into you! I would you had half the courage and spirit this Señor Zorro has! He has principles and he fights for them. He aids the helpless and avenges the oppressed. I salute him! I would rather have you, my son, risking your life as he does, than to have you a lifeless dreamer of dreams that amount to nothing!"

"My father! I have been a dutiful son."

"I wish you had been a little wild—it would have been more natural." Don Alejandro sighed. "I could overlook a few escapades more easily than I can lifelessness. Wake up, young sir! Remember that you are a Vega. When I was your age, I was not a laughingstock. I was ready to fight at a wink, to make love to every pair of flashing eyes. Ha!"

"I pray you, do not 'Ha!' me, father. My nerves are on edge."

"You must be more of a man."

"I will attempt it immediately," Don Diego said, straightening himself somewhat in his chair. "I had hoped to avoid it, but it appears that I cannot. I will court the Señorita Lolita as other men court maidens. You meant what you said about your fortune?"

"I did," said Don Alejandro.

"Then I must act. It would never do, of course, to let that fortune go out of the family. I shall think these matters over in peace and quiet tonight. Perhaps I can meditate here, far from the pueblo. By the saints!"

The last exclamation was caused by a sudden commotion outside the house. Don Alejandro and his son heard a number of horsemen stop, heard their calls to one another, heard bridles jingling and blades rattling.

"There is no peace in all the world," Don Diego said gloomily.

A servant opened the door, and into the great room there strode ten caballeros, with blades at their sides and pistols in their belts.

"Ha, Don Alejandro! We ask your hospitality!" the one of them cried.

"You have it without asking, caballeros. Where are you riding?"

"We pursue Señor Zorro, the highwayman."

"By the saints!" Don Diego cried. "One cannot escape it even here. Violence and bloodshed!"

"He invaded the plaza at Reina de Los Angeles," the spokesman went on. "He had the magistrate whipped because he sentenced Friar Felipe to receive the lash, and he whipped the fat landlord. Then he rode away, and we are pursuing him. He has been in the area?"

"Not to my knowledge," Don Alejandro said. "My son arrived off the highway a short time ago."

"You did not see the fellow, Don Diego?"

"Fortunately, I did not," Don Diego said.

Don Alejandro had sent for servants, and now wine mugs were on the long table and heaps of small cakes. The caballeros began to eat and drink. Don Diego knew what that meant. Their pursuit of the highwayman was at an end. They would sit at his father's table and drink throughout the night and shout and sing and tell stories. And in the morning ride back to Reina de Los Angeles like so many heroes.

It was the custom. The chase of Señor Zorro was just an excuse for a merry time.

The servants brought great stone jugs filled with rare wine and put them on the table. Don Alejandro ordered that meat be fetched also. The young caballeros liked these parties at Don Alejandro's. The don's good wife had been dead for several years, and there were no women except servants, and so they could make what noise they pleased throughout the night.

They put aside pistols and blades and began to boast and brag. Don Alejandro had his servants put the weapons in a far corner out of the way, for he did not wish a drunken quarrel, with a dead caballero or two in his house.

Don Diego drank and talked with them for a time, and then sat to one side and listened, as if such foolishness bored him.

"It is a good thing for this Señor Zorro that we did not catch up with him," one cried. "Any one of us is a match for the fellow."

"Ha, for a chance at him!" another screeched. "How the landlord did howl when he was whipped!"

"He rode in this direction?" Don Alejandro asked.

"We are not sure of that. He took the San Gabriel trail, and thirty of us followed. We separated into three bands, each going a different direction. It is the good fortune of one of the other bands to have him now, I suppose. But it is our excellent good fortune to be here."

Don Diego stood before the company.

"Señores, I ask your pardon," he said. "I am exhausted from the journey and must go to bed."

"Certainly," one of his friends cried. "And when you are rested, come out to us again and make merry."

They laughed at that. Don Diego bowed, then hurried from the room.

He entered a room that always was ready for him and closed the door behind him. Bernardo stretched his big form on the floor just outside it, to guard his master during the night.

In the great living room, Don Diego scarcely was missed. His father was frowning and twisting his mustache, for he would have had his son like other young men. He sighed and wished that the saints had given him a son with red blood in his veins.

The caballeros were singing now, joining in the chorus of a popular love song, and their discordant voices filled the big room. Don Alejandro smiled as he listened, for it brought his own youth back to him.

They sprawled on chairs and benches on both sides of the long table, pounding it with their mugs as they sang, laughing loudly now and then.

"If only Señor Zorro were here now!" one of them cried.

A voice from the doorway answered him:

"Señores, he is here!"

CHAPTER 25

A League Is Formed

The song ceased; the laughter was stilled. They blinked their eyes and looked across the room. Señor Zorro stood just inside the door, having entered from the veranda. He wore his long cloak and his mask. In one hand he held a pistol, and its muzzle was pointed at the table.

"So these are the sort of men who pursue Señor Zorro and hope to take him," he said. "Do not move, señores. I see that your weapons are in the corner. I could kill some of you and be gone before you could reach them. Your noise may be heard a mile away, señores. Is this the way you attend to duty? Why have you stopped to make merry while Señor Zorro rides the highway?"

"Give me my blade and let me stand before him!" one cried.

"You are barely able to stand, señor," the highwayman answered. "Do you think there is one of you who could fence with me now?"

"There is one!" cried Don Alejandro, in a loud voice, springing to his feet. "I openly say that I have admired some of the things you have done, señor. But now you have entered my house and are abusing my guests, and I must call you to account!"

"I have no quarrel with you, Don Alejandro, and you have none with me," Señor Zorro said. "I refuse to cross blades with you. And I am but telling these men some truths."

"By the saints, I will make you!"

"A moment, Don Alejandro! Señores, this aged don would fight me, and that would mean a wound or death for him. Will you allow it?"

"Don Alejandro must not fight our battles!" one of them cried.

"Then see that he sits in his place, and all honor to him."

Don Alejandro started forward, but two of the caballeros sprang before him and urged him to go back, saying that his honor was safe, since he offered combat. Raging, Don Alejandro complied.

"A worthy bunch of young men," Señor Zorro sneered. "You drink wine and make merry while injustice is all around you. Take your swords in hand and attack oppression! Live up to your noble names and your blue blood, señores! Drive the thieving politicians from the land! Protect the friars whose work gave us these broad acres! Be men, not drunken fashion plates!"

"By the saints!" one cried and sprang to his feet.

"Back, or I fire! I have not come here to fight you in Don Alejandro's house. I respect him too much for that. I have come to tell you these truths concerning yourselves. Your families can make or break a governor! Band yourselves together in a good cause, caballeros, and make some use of your lives. You would do it, were you not afraid. You seek adventure? Here is adventure a plenty, fighting injustice."

"By the saints, it would be a lark!" cried one in answer.

"Look upon it as a lark if it pleases you, yet you would be doing some good. Would the politicians dare stand against you, sons of the most powerful families? Band yourselves together and give yourselves a name. Make yourselves feared throughout the land."

"It would be treason—"

"It is not treason to take down a tyrant, caballeros! Is it that you are afraid?"

"By the saints—no!" they cried.

"Then make your stand!"

"You would lead us?"

"*Si*, señores!"

"Are you of good blood?"

"I am a caballero, of blood as good as any here," Señor Zorro told them.

"Your name? Where does your family live?"

"Those things must remain secrets for the present. I have given you my word."

"Your face—"

"Must remain masked for the time being, señores."

They had lurched to their feet now and were shouting their approval.

"Wait!" one cried. "This is an imposition upon Don Alejandro. He may not be in sympathy, and we are planning and plotting in his house—"

"I am in sympathy, caballeros, and give you my support," Don Alejandro said.

Their cheers filled the great room. None could stand against them if Don Alejandro Vega was with them. Not even the governor himself would dare oppose them.

"It is a bargain!" they cried. "We will call ourselves the Avengers! We will ride El Camino Real and prove terrors to those who rob honest men and mistreat Indians! We will drive the thieving politicians out!"

"And then you will be caballeros in truth, knights protecting the weak," Señor Zorro said. "You will never regret this decision, señores! I lead, and I give you loyalty and expect as much. Also, I expect obedience to orders. We will keep our existence a secret for now. In the morning return to Reina de Los Angeles and say you did not find Señor Zorro—say rather that you did not catch him, which will be the truth. Be ready to band yourselves together and ride. I will send word when the time arrives. I know you all. I will get word to one, and he can inform the others. It is agreed?"

"Agreed!" they shouted.

"Then I will leave you for now. You are to remain in this room, and none is to try to follow me. It is a command. *Buenos noches,* caballeros!" He bowed before them, swung the door open, and darted through it, slamming it shut behind him.

They could hear the clatter of a horse's hoofs on the driveway. And then they raised their wine mugs and drank to their new league and to Señor Zorro, the Curse of Capistrano, and to Don Alejandro Vega. They sat down again and began speaking of wrongs that should be righted, each of them knowing half a dozen.

Don Alejandro Vega sat in one corner, by himself, a grief-stricken man because his only son was asleep in the house and had not red blood enough to take a part in such an undertaking.

As if to add to his misery, Don Diego at that moment came slowly into the room, rubbing his eyes and yawning and looking as if he had been disturbed.

"It is impossible for a man to sleep in this house tonight," he said. "Give me a mug of wine, and I shall take my place with you. What was the cheering about?"

"Señor Zorro has been here—" his father began.

"The highwayman? Been here? By the saints! It is as much as a man can endure."

"Sit down, my son," Don Alejandro urged. "Certain things have happened. There will be a chance now for you to show what sort of blood flows in your veins."

Don Alejandro's manner was very determined.

CHAPTER 26

An Understanding

The remainder of the night was spent by the caballeros in making plans to be submitted to Señor Zorro for his approval. Though they appeared to look on this as a means to adventure, yet there was an undercurrent of seriousness in their manner. They realized that things were not as they should be, and in reality they were ones who could bring fairness to all. They had thought of these things often, but had made no move because they had not been banded together and had no leader. Each young caballero had waited for another to start the thing. But now Señor Zorro had struck at the psychological moment, and things could be done.

Don Diego was told what had happened. His father informed him that he was to play a part and prove himself a man. Don Diego fumed considerably and declared that such a thing would cause his death, yet he would do it for his father's sake.

Early in the morning after a hearty meal, the caballeros started back to Reina de Los Angeles.

Don Diego rode with them at his father's order. Nothing was to be said about their plans. They were to get recruits from the remainder of the thirty who had set out in pursuit of Señor Zorro. Some would join them readily, they knew, while others were the governor's men pure and simple, and would have to be kept in the dark.

They rode leisurely, for which Don Diego remarked that he was grateful. Bernardo was still following him on the mule. Bernardo knew something momentous was being planned, but could not guess what.

When they reached the plaza, they found that the other two parties already were there, saying that they had not come up with the highwayman. Some declared that they had seen him in the distance, and one that he had fired a pistol at him.

Don Diego left his companions and hurried to his house, where he put on fresh clothing. Then he ordered his carriage around. That carriage was one of the most gorgeous along El Camino Real. Why Don Diego had purchased it had always been a mystery. There were some who said he did it to show his wealth, while others declared a manufacturer's agent had pestered him so much that Don Diego had given him the order to be rid of him.

Don Diego came from his house dressed in his best; but he did not get into the carriage. Again there was a commotion in the plaza, and into it rode Sergeant Pedro Gonzales and his troopers. The man Captain Ramón had sent after them had overtaken them easily, for they had been riding slowly and had not covered many miles.

"Ha, Don Diego, my friend!" Gonzales cried. "Still living in this turbulent world?"

"From necessity," Don Diego replied. "Did you capture this Señor Zorro?"

"The pretty bird escaped us, caballero. It appears that he turned toward San Gabriel that night, while we went chasing him toward Pala. Ah, well, it does not matter. Our revenge will be the greater when we find him."

"What will you do next, my sergeant?"

"My men refresh themselves, and then we ride toward San Gabriel. It is said the highwayman is in that vicinity, though some thirty young men of blood failed to find him last night after he had caused the magistrate to be whipped. No doubt he hid himself in the brush and chuckled when the caballeros rode by."

"May your horse have speed and your sword arm strength," Don Diego said and got into his carriage.

Two magnificent horses were hitched to the carriage, and a coachman drove them. Don Diego stretched back on the cushions and half closed his eyes as the carriage started. The driver went across the plaza, turned into the highway, and started toward the Hacienda of Don Carlos Pulido.

Sitting on his veranda, Don Carlos saw the gorgeous carriage approaching, and growled low down in his throat. Then he got up and hurried into the house, to face his wife and daughter.

"Señorita, Don Diego comes," he said. "I have spoken to you about the young man. I trust that you have thought about him as a dutiful daughter should."

Then he turned and went out to the veranda again, and the señorita rushed into her room and threw herself upon a couch to weep. The saints knew she wished that she could feel some love for Don Diego and take him for a husband, for it would help her father's fortunes. Yet she felt that she could not.

Why did the man not act like a caballero? Why did he not show some measure of common sense? Why did he insist on acting like an aged don with one foot in the grave?

Don Diego got from the carriage and waved to the driver to continue to the stable yard. He greeted Don Carlos lifelessly. Don Carlos was surprised to note that Don Diego had a guitar beneath one arm. He put the guitar down on the floor, removed his sombrero, and sighed. "I have been out to see my father," he said.

"Ha! Don Alejandro is well, I hope?"

"He is in excellent health, as usual. He has instructed me to persist in my suit for the Señorita Lolita's hand. If I do not win me a wife within a certain time, he says, he will give his fortune to the Franciscans when he passes away."

"Indeed?"

"My father is not a man to waste his words. Don Carlos, I must win the señorita. I know of no other young woman who would be as acceptable to my father as a daughter-in-law."

"A little wooing, Don Diego, I beg of you. Be not so matter-of-fact, I pray."

"I have decided to woo as other men, though it no doubt will be much of a bore. How would you suggest that I start?"

"It is difficult to give advice in such a case," Don Carlos replied, trying desperately to remember how he had done it when he had courted Doña Catalina. "It might be an excellent thing to look at the señorita as if you adored her. Say nothing about marriage at first, but speak rather of love. Try to talk in low, rich tones, and say those meaningless nothings in which a young woman can find a world of meaning. It is a gentle art—saying one thing and meaning another."

"I fear that it is beyond me," Don Diego said. "Yet I must try, of course. I may see the señorita now?"

Don Carlos went to the doorway and called his wife and daughter. Doña Catalina smiled upon Don Diego in encouragement. Señorita Lolita smiled also, yet with fear and trembling. For she had given her heart to the unknown

Señor Zorro and could love no other man. She could not wed a man she did not love, not even to save her father from poverty.

Don Diego led the señorita to a bench at one end of the veranda and started to talk of things in general, plucking at the strings of the guitar as he did so. Don Carlos and his wife removed themselves to the other end of the veranda and hoped that things would go well.

Señorita Lolita was glad that Don Diego did not speak of marriage as he had done before. Instead, he told of what had happened in the pueblo, of Friar Felipe's whipping, and of how Señor Zorro had punished the magistrate and fought a dozen men and made his escape. Despite his air of exhaustion, Don Diego spoke in an interesting manner, and the señorita found herself liking him more than before.

He told, too, of how he had gone to his father's hacienda.

"My father threatens to disinherit me if I do not get my wife within a specified time," Don Diego said then. "Would you like to see me lose my father's estate, señorita?"

"Certainly not," she replied. "There are many girls who would be proud to marry you, Don Diego."

"But not you?"

"Certainly, I would be proud. But can a girl help it if her heart does not speak? Would you want a wife who did not love you? Think of the long years you would have to spend beside her, and no love to make them endurable."

"You do not think, then, that you ever could learn to love me, señorita?"

Suddenly the girl faced him and spoke in low, earnest tones.

"You are a caballero of the blood, señor. I may trust you?"

"To death, señorita."

"Then I have something to tell you. And I ask that you let it remain your secret. It is an explanation in a way."

"Proceed, señorita."

"If my heart told me do so, nothing would please me more than to become your wife, señor. But perhaps I am too honest to wed where I do not love. There is one great reason why I cannot love you."

"There is some other man in your heart?"

"You have guessed it, señor. My heart is filled with his image. You would not want me for wife in such case. My parents do not know. You must keep my secret. I swear by the saints that I have spoken the truth."

"The man is worthy?"

"I feel sure that he is, caballero. You understand now?"

"I understand fully, señorita. May I express the hope that you will find him worthy and in time the man of your choice?"

"I knew you would be the true caballero."

"And if you need a friend, call on me, señorita."

"My father must not suspect at the present time. We must let him think that you still seek me, and I will pretend to be thinking more of you than before. And gradually you can cease your visits—"

"I understand, señorita. Yet that leaves me in a difficult situation. I have asked your father for permission to woo you, and if I go to wooing another girl now, I will bring his anger down on myself. And if I do not woo another girl, I will have my own father angry with me. It is a sorry state."

"Perhaps it will not be for long, señor."

"Ha! I have it! What does a man do when he is disappointed in love? He mopes, he pulls a long face, he refuses to partake of the actions and excitements of the times. Señorita, you have saved me in a way. I shall sorrow because you do not return my love. Then men will think they know the reason when I dream in the sun and meditate instead of riding and fighting like a fool. I will be allowed to go my way in peace. An excellent thought!"

"Señor, you are amazing!" the Señorita Lolita exclaimed, laughing.

Don Carlos and Doña Catalina heard that laugh, looked around, and then exchanged quick

glances. Don Diego Vega was getting along famously with the señorita, they thought.

Then Don Diego continued the deception by playing his guitar and singing a verse of a song that had to do with bright eyes and love. Don Carlos and his wife glanced at each other again, this time in apprehension. They wished that he would stop, for he was not much of a musician or vocalist, and they feared that he might lose what ground he had gained in the señorita's estimation.

But Lolita did not act displeased. There was some more conversation, and just before the siesta hour Don Diego bade them *buenos dias* and rode away in his gorgeous carriage. From the turn in the driveway, he waved back at them.

CHAPTER 27

Orders for Arrest

Captain Ramón's courier, sent north with the letter for the governor, had dreams of good times in San Francisco de Asis before returning to his presidio at Reina de Los Angeles. He knew a certain señorita there whose beauty caused his heart to burn.

So he rode like a fiend after leaving his commandant's office, changed horses at San Fernando and at a hacienda along the way. He galloped into Santa Barbara just at dusk, with the intention of changing horses again, getting meat and bread and wine at the presidio, and rushing on his way.

And at Santa Barbara his hopes of basking in the señorita's smiles at San Francisco de Asis were cruelly shattered. For before the door of the presidio there was a gorgeous carriage that made Don Diego's appear like a mere horse cart. Twenty horses were tethered there, and more troopers than usual moved about the highway, laughing and joking with one another.

The governor was in Santa Barbara.

His excellency had left San Francisco de Asis some days before on a trip of inspection. He intended to go as far south as San Diego de Alcala, strengthening his political fences, rewarding his friends, and punishing his enemies.

He had reached Santa Barbara an hour before and was listening to the report of the commandant there. He planned to spend the night at the house of a friend. His troopers would be given quarters at the presidio, and the journey was to continue the next morning.

Captain Ramón's courier had been told that the letter he carried was of the utmost importance, and so he hurried to the office of the commandant.

"I come from Captain Ramón, commandant at Reina de Los Angeles, with a letter of importance for His Excellency," he reported, standing stiffly at attention.

The governor grunted and took the letter, and the commandant motioned for the courier to withdraw. His excellency read the letter. When he had finished there was an unholy gleam in his eyes, and he twirled his mustache with keen satisfaction. Then he read the letter again and frowned.

He liked the thought that he could crush Don Carlos Pulido more, but he disliked the thought that Señor Zorro was still at liberty. He got up and paced the floor for a time, and then whirled upon the commandant.

"I shall leave for the south at sunrise," he said. "My presence is urgently needed at Reina de Los Angeles. You will attend to things. Tell that courier he will ride back with my escort. I go now to the house of my friend."

And so, in the morning, the governor started south, his escort of twenty picked troopers surrounding him, the courier in their midst. He traveled swiftly. On a certain day at midmorning he entered the plaza of Reina de Los Angeles. It was the same morning that Don Diego rode to the Pulido hacienda in his carriage, taking his guitar with him.

The carriage and soldiers stopped before the tavern. The fat landlord almost suffered heart failure because he had not been warned of the governor's coming and was afraid he would enter the inn and find it in a dirty state.

But the governor made no effort to leave his carriage and enter the tavern. He was glancing around the square, observing many things. He never felt secure concerning the men of rank in this pueblo. He felt that he did not have the proper grip on them.

He watched carefully as news of his arrival was spread and certain caballeros hurried to the plaza to greet him and make him welcome. He noted those who appeared to be sincere, observed those who were in no particular haste to salute him, and noticed that several were absent.

Business must receive his first attention, he told them, and he must hasten up to the presidio. After that he would gladly be the guest of any of them. He accepted an invitation and ordered his driver to proceed. He was remembering Captain Ramón's letter, and he had not seen Don Diego Vega in the plaza.

Sergeant Gonzales and his men were away pursuing Señor Zorro, of course, so Captain Ramón himself was awaiting his excellency at the presidio entrance. He saluted the governor gravely, and bowed low before him and ordered the commander of the escort to take charge of the place.

He led his excellency to the private office, and the governor sat down.

"What is the latest news?" he asked.

"My men are on the trail, Excellency. But, as I wrote, this pest of a Señor Zorro has friends. My sergeant has reported that twice he found him with a band of followers."

"They must be broken up, killed off!" the governor cried. "A man of that sort always can get followers, and yet more followers, until he will be so strong that he can cause us serious trouble. Has he committed any further atrocities?"

"He has, Excellency. Yesterday a friar from San Gabriel was whipped for swindling. Señor

Zorro caught the witnesses against him on the highroad and whipped them almost to death. And then he rode into the pueblo just at dusk and had the magistrate whipped. My soldiers were away looking for him at the time. It appears that this Señor Zorro knows the movements of my force and always strikes where the troopers are not."

"Then spies are giving him warnings?"

"It appears so, Excellency. Last night some thirty young caballeros rode after him but did not find the scoundrel. They returned this morning."

"Was Don Diego Vega with them?"

"He did not ride out with them, but he returned with them. It seems that they picked him up at his father's hacienda. You perhaps guessed that I meant the Vegas in my letter. I am convinced now, Your Excellency, that my suspicions concerning him were unjust. This Señor Zorro even invaded Don Diego's house one night while Don Diego was away."

"How is this?"

"But Don Carlos Pulido and his family were there."

"Ha! In Don Diego's house? What is the meaning of that?"

"It is amusing," said Captain Ramón, laughing lightly. "I have heard that Don Alejandro ordered Don Diego to get a wife. The young man is not the sort to woo women. He is lifeless."

"I know the man. Proceed."

"So he rides straightway to the Hacienda of Don Carlos and asks permission to court Don Carlos's only daughter. Don Diego asked Don Carlos to come to the pueblo with his family, where it would be safer from Señor Zorro. Don Diego wanted them to stay at his house until he returned from his hacienda. The Pulidos could not refuse, of course. And Señor Zorro, it appears, followed them."

"Ha! Go on."

"It is laughable that Don Diego fetched them here to escape Señor Zorro's wrath, when, in reality, they are hand in glove with the highwayman. Remember, this Señor Zorro had been at the Pulido hacienda. We got word from a servant and almost caught him there. He had been eating a meal. He was hiding in a closet, and while I was alone there and my men searching the trails, he came from the closet, ran me through the shoulder from behind, and escaped."

"The low scoundrel!" the governor exclaimed. "But do you think there will be a marriage between Don Diego and the Señorita Pulido?"

"I imagine there need be no worry about that, Excellency. I imagine that Don Diego's father called his son's attention to the fact that Don Carlos does not stand very high with Your Excellency and that there are daughters of other men who do. At any rate, after the Pulidos left, Don Diego called upon me here at the presidio and appeared to be anxious that I would not think him a man of treason."

"I am glad to hear it! The Vegas are powerful. They never have been my warm friends, yet never have they raised hands against me, so I cannot complain. It is good sense to keep them friendly, if that is possible. But these Pulidos—"

"Even the señorita appears to be giving aid to this highwayman," Captain Ramón said. "She boasted to me of what she called his courage. She sneered at the soldiers. Don Carlos Pulido and some of the friars are protecting the man, giving him food and drink, hiding him, sending him news of the troopers' whereabouts. The Pulidos are hindering our efforts to capture the rogue. I would have taken steps, but I thought it best to inform you and await your decision."

"There can be but one decision in such a case," said the governor loftily. "No matter how good a man's blood may be, he cannot be allowed to commit treason without suffering the consequences. I had thought that Don Carlos had learned his lesson, but it appears that he has not. Are any of your men in the presidio?"

"Some who are ill, Excellency."

"That courier of yours returned with my escort. Does he know the country well hereabouts?"

"Certainly, Excellency."

"Then he can act as guide. Send half my escort to the Hacienda of Don Carlos Pulido at once. Have them arrest the don and bring him to jail and imprison him there. That will be a blow to his high blood. I have had quite enough of these Pulidos."

"And the haughty doña, who sneered at me, and the proud señorita who scorned the troopers?"

"Ha! It is a good thought. It will teach a lesson to all in this locality. Have them brought to jail and imprisoned also," the governor said.

CHAPTER 28

The Outrage

Don Diego's carriage had just pulled up before his house when a squad of troopers went by it in a cloud of dust. He did not recognize any of them.

"Ha! Are there new soldiers on the trail of Señor Zorro?" he asked a man standing near.

"They are a part of the escort of the governor, caballero."

"The governor is here?"

"He arrived but a short time ago, caballero, and has gone to the presidio."

"I suppose they must have fresh news of this highwayman to send them riding furiously through dust and sun like that. He appears to be an elusive rascal. By the saints! Had I been here when the governor arrived, no doubt he would have put up at my house. Now some other caballero will have the honor of entertaining him. It is to be much regretted."

And then Don Diego went into the house, and the man who had heard him speak did not know whether to doubt the sincerity of that last remark.

Led by the courier, who knew the way, the squad of troopers galloped swiftly along the highroad, and soon turned up the trail toward Don Carlos's house. As they struck the driveway, they scattered to left and right, tearing up Doña Catalina's flowerbeds and sending chickens squawking out of the way, and so surrounded the house in almost an instant of time.

Don Carlos had been sitting on the veranda in his accustomed place, half-dozing. He did not notice the advance of the troopers until he heard the beating of their horses' hoofs. He got to his feet in alarm, wondering whether Señor Zorro was in the vicinity again and the soldiers after him. Three dismounted in a cloud of dust before the steps, and the sergeant who commanded them made his way forward, slapping the dust from his uniform.

"You are Don Carlos Pulido?" he asked in a loud voice.

"I am, señor."

"I have orders to place you under military arrest."

"Arrest!" Don Carlos cried. "Who gave you such orders?"

"His excellency, the governor. He now is in Reina de Los Angeles, señor."

"And the charge?"

"Treason and aiding the enemies of the state."

"Preposterous!" Don Carlos cried. "I am accused of treason? What are the particulars of the charges?"

"You will have to ask the magistrate that, señor. I know nothing of the matter except that I am to arrest you."

"You wish me to accompany you?"

"I demand it, señor."

"I am a man of blood, a caballero—"

"I have my orders."

"So I cannot be trusted to appear at my place of trial? But perhaps the hearing is to be held immediately. So much the better, for the quicker can I clear myself. We go to the presidio?"

"I go to the presidio when this work is done. You go to jail," the sergeant said.

"To jail?" Don Carlos screeched. "You would dare? You would throw a caballero into the filthy jail?"

"I have my orders, señor. You will prepare to accompany us at once."

"I must give my superintendent instructions regarding the management of the hacienda."

"I'll go along with you, señor."

Don Carlos's face flamed purple. His hands clenched as he looked at the sergeant.

"Am I to be insulted with every word?" he cried. "Do you think I would run away like a criminal?"

"I have my orders, señor," the sergeant said.

"At least I may break this news to my wife and daughter without an outsider being at my shoulder?"

"Your wife is Doña Catalina Pulido?"

"Certainly."

"I am ordered to arrest her also, señor."

"Scum!" Don Carlos cried. "You would put hands on a lady? You would remove her from her house?"

"Those are my orders. She, too, is charged with treason and with aiding the enemies of the state."

"By the saints! It is too much! I shall fight against you and your men as long as there is breath in my body!"

"And that will not be for long, Don Carlos, if you attempt to give battle. I am but carrying out my orders."

"My beloved wife placed under arrest! And on such a charge! What are you to do with her, Sergeant?"

"She goes to jail."

"My wife in that foul place? Is there no justice in the land? She is a tender lady of noble blood—"

"Enough of this, señor. My orders are my orders, and I carry them out as instructed. I am a soldier and I obey."

Now Doña Catalina came running to the veranda, for she had been listening to the conversation just inside the door. Her face was white, but there was a look of pride in it. She feared Don Carlos might attack the soldier, and she feared he would be wounded or slain if he did.

"You have heard?" Don Carlos asked.

"I have heard, my husband. It is just more persecution. I am too proud to argue the point with these common soldiers. They are just carrying out their orders. A Pulido can be a Pulido, my husband, even in a foul jail."

"But the shame of it!" Don Carlos cried. "What does it all mean? Where will it end? And our daughter will be here alone with the servants."

"Your daughter is Señorita Lolita Pulido?" the sergeant asked. "Then do not grieve, señor, for you will not be separated. I have an order for the arrest of your daughter, also."

"The charge?"

"The same, señor."

"And you would take her—"

"To jail."

"An innocent, high-born, gentle girl?"

"My orders, señor," said the sergeant.

"May the saints blast the man who issued them!" Don Carlos cried. "They have taken my wealth and lands. They have heaped shame upon my family. But, thank the saints, they cannot break our pride!"

And then Don Carlos took his wife by the

arm and turned to enter the house, with the sergeant at his heels. He broke the news to the Señorita Lolita, who stood speechless for an instant, and then burst into a torrent of tears. Then the pride of the Pulidos came to her. She dried her eyes and looked with scorn at the big sergeant and pulled aside her skirts when he stepped near.

Servants brought the cart to the door, and Don Carlos and his wife and daughter got into it. The journey of shame to the pueblo began.

Their hearts might be bursting with grief, but not one of the Pulidos showed it. They held their heads high, looked straight ahead, and pretended not to hear the low taunts of the soldiers.

They passed others, who were crowded off the road by the troopers, and who looked with wonder at those in the cart, but they did not speak. Some watched in sorrow, and some grinned at the sight.

Finally, the cart came to the edge of Reina de Los Angeles. There the family met fresh insult. His excellency had decided that the Pulidos should be humbled to the dust. He had sent some of his troopers to spread news of what was being done and to give coins to Indians and laborers if they would jeer the prisoners when they arrived. The governor wished to teach a lesson that would prevent other noble families from turning against him and wished it to appear that the Pulidos were hated by all classes alike.

At the edge of the plaza they were met by the mob. There were cruel taunts, some of which no innocent señorita should have heard. Don Carlos's face was red with wrath. There were tears in Doña Catalina's eyes. Señorita Lolita's lips were trembling. But they gave no other sign that they heard.

The drive around the plaza to the jail was made slow purposely. One man threw mud, and it splashed on Don Carlos's breast, but he refused to notice it. He had one arm around his wife, the other around his daughter, as if to give them what protection he could. He was looking straight ahead.

There were some men of blood who witnessed the scene, but they did not take part in the uproar. Some of them were as old as Don Carlos, and this thing brought to their hearts fresh hatred of the governor.

And some were young, with the blood running hot in their veins. They looked upon the suffering face of Doña Catalina and imagined her their own mother, and upon the lovely face of the señorita and imagined her their sister or fiancée.

And some of these men glanced at one another furtively. Though they did not speak they were wondering the same thing—whether Señor Zorro would hear of this. Whether he would send word around for the members of the new league to gather.

The cart stopped in front of the jail finally, with the shouting mob surrounding it. The soldiers made some pretense of holding them back. The sergeant dismounted and forced Don Carlos and his wife and daughter to step to the ground.

Crude and drunken men jostled them as they walked up the steps to the door. More mud was thrown, and some of it spattered upon Doña Catalina's gown. But if the mob expected an outburst on the part of the aged caballero, it was disappointed. Don Carlos held his head high, ignoring the mob, and so led the ladies to the door.

The sergeant beat against it with the heavy hilt of his sword. A small window was opened, and in it appeared the evil, grinning face of the jailer.

"What have we here?" he demanded.

"Three prisoners charged with treason," the sergeant replied.

The door was thrown open. There came a last burst of jeers from the mob. Then the prisoners were inside, and the door had been closed and bolted again.

The jailer led the way along an evil-smelling hall and threw open another door.

"In with you," he directed.

The three prisoners were thrust inside, and this door was closed and barred. They blinked their eyes in the semi-gloom. Gradually they made out two windows, some benches, some human derelicts sprawled against the walls.

They had not even been given the courtesy of a clean, private room. Don Carlos and his wife and daughter had been thrust in with the scum of the pueblo, with drunkards and thieves and dishonored women.

They sat down on a bench in one corner of the room, as far from the others as possible. And then Doña Catalina and her daughter gave way to tears, and tears streamed down the face of the aged don as he tried to comfort them.

"I would to the saints that Don Diego Vega were my son-in-law now," the don breathed.

His daughter pressed his arm.

"Perhaps—my father—a friend will come," she whispered. "Perhaps the evil man who caused this suffering will be punished."

For it seemed to the señorita that a vision of Señor Zorro had appeared before her; and she had great faith in the man to whom she had given her love.

CHAPTER 29

Don Diego Feels Ill

One hour after the jail door closed behind Don Carlos Pulido and his family, Don Diego Vega made his way slowly on foot up the slope to the presidio to make his call on his excellency, the governor.

He walked with swinging stride, gazing to right and left as if at the hills in the distance. Once he stopped to observe a blossom that bloomed beside the path. He was elegantly dressed. His sword was at his side, his most fashionable one with its jeweled hilt. In his right hand he carried a handkerchief of flimsy lace, which he wafted this way and that, and now and then touched it to the tip of his nose.

He bowed ceremoniously to two or three caballeros who passed him, but spoke to none beyond the necessary words of greeting, and they did not seek conversation with him. For, knowing that Don Diego Vega was courting the daughter of Don Carlos, they wondered how he would react to her imprisonment along with her father and mother. They did not care to discuss the matter, for their own feelings were high, and they feared they might say things that could be considered treason.

Don Diego came to the front door of the presidio. The sergeant in charge called the soldiers to attention and saluted the caballero. Don Diego answered with a wave of his hand and a smile, and went on to the commandant's office, where the governor was receiving such caballeros as cared to call and express their loyalty.

He greeted his excellency with carefully chosen words, bowed, and then took the chair the governor was kind enough to indicate.

"Don Diego Vega," the governor said, "I am doubly glad that you have called on me today. In these times a man who holds high office would know his friends."

"I should have called sooner, but I was away from my house at the time you arrived," Don Diego said. "Do you plan to remain long in Reina de Los Angeles, Excellency?"

"Until this highwayman, known as Señor Zorro, is either slain or taken," the governor said.

"By the saints! Am I never to hear the last of that rogue?" Don Diego cried. "I have heard of nothing else for days. I go to spend an evening with a friar, and in comes a crowd of soldiers chasing this Señor Zorro. I go to the hacienda of my father to get me peace and quiet, and along comes a crowd of caballeros seeking news of Señor Zorro. These are turbulent times. A man whose nature inclines him to music and the poets has no right to exist in the present age."

"I am sorry that you have been annoyed," the governor said, laughing. "But I hope to have the fellow soon, and so put an end to that particular annoyance. Captain Ramón has sent for his big sergeant and his troopers to return. I brought an escort of twenty. And so we have ample men to run down this Curse of Capistrano when next he makes his appearance."

"Let us hope it will end as it should," said Don Diego.

"A man in high office has many things with which to contend," the governor went on. "Look at what I was forced to do this day. I am called upon to put in prison a man of good blood and his wife and tender daughter. But the state must be protected."

"I suppose you mean Don Carlos Pulido and his family?"

"I do, caballero."

"This reminds me that I must say a few words regarding that," Don Diego said. "I am wondering if my honor is involved."

"Why, caballero, how can that be?"

"My father has ordered that I get me a wife. Some days ago I requested of Don Carlos Pulido permission to court his daughter."

"Ha! I understand. But you are not the fiancé of the young lady?"

"Not yet, Excellency."

"Then your honor is not involved, Don Diego, that I can see."

"But I have been visiting to her."

"You may thank the saints that it has gone no further, Don Diego. Think how it would look if you were allied with this family now. As for getting you a wife—come north with me to San Francisco de Asis, caballero, where the señoritas are far more lovely than here in your southland. Look over those of good blood, and let me know your preference, and I'll guarantee that the lady will listen to your suit and accept your hand and name. I can guarantee, also, that she will be of a loyal family. We shall get you a wife of the proper sort, caballero."

"If you will pardon me, is it not taking stern measures to have Don Carlos and his ladies thrown into the jail?" Don Diego asked, flicking dust from his sleeve.

"I find it necessary, señor."

"Do you think it will add to your popularity, Excellency?"

"Whether it does or not, the state must be served."

"Men of good blood hate to see such a thing. There may be murmurings," Don Diego warned. "I should hate to see your excellency make a wrong step at this point."

"What do you think I should do?" the governor asked.

"Place Don Carlos and the ladies under house arrest, if you will, but do not put them in the jail. It is unnecessary; they will not run away. Bring them to trial as gentle folk should be brought to trial."

"You are bold, caballero."

"By the saints, am I talking too much?"

"It is better to leave these matters to the few of us who are trusted with the responsibility," the governor said. "I can understand, of course, how it upsets a man of good blood to see a don thrown into a jail, and to see his ladies treated likewise, but in such a case as this—"

"I have not heard the nature of the case," Don Diego said.

"Ha! Perhaps you may change your mind when you hear it. You have been speaking of this Señor Zorro. What if I tell you that the highwayman is being protected and fed by Don Carlos Pulido?"

"That is astonishing!"

"And that the Doña Catalina is a party to the treason? And that the lovely señorita has seen fit to talk treasonably and dip her pretty hands into a conspiracy against the state?"

"This is past belief!" Don Diego cried.

"Some nights ago Señor Zorro was at the

Pulido hacienda. Don Carlos aided the bandit and hid him in a closet. When Captain Ramón was there alone, this highwayman stepped from the closet and attacked him treacherously and wounded him."

"By the saints!"

"And while you were gone and the Pulidos were your house guests, Señor Zorro was in your house, speaking to the señorita, when the commandant walked in upon them. And the señorita grasped Captain Ramón by the arm and pestered him until Señor Zorro had escaped."

"It is unbelievable!" Don Diego exclaimed.

"Captain Ramón has given me other evidence too. Can you wonder now that I had them placed in jail? If I merely put them under arrest, this Señor Zorro would help them escape."

"And your intentions, Excellency?"

"I shall keep them in jail while my troopers run down this highwayman. I will force him to confess and implicate them—and then they will have a trial."

"These turbulent times!" Don Diego complained.

"As a loyal man—and I hope an admirer of mine—you should hope to see foes of the state overcome."

"I do. Most sincerely do I. All real foes of the state should receive punishment."

"I am glad to hear you say that, caballero!"

the governor cried, and he reached across the table and grasped Don Diego fervently by the hand.

There was some more talk that amounted to nothing. Then Don Diego took his leave, for there were other men waiting to see the governor. After he had left the office the governor looked across at Captain Ramón and smiled.

"You are right, commandant," he said. "Such a man could not be a traitor. It would tire him too much to think treasonable thoughts. What a man! He must be enough to drive that old fire-eater of a father of his insane."

Don Diego made his way slowly down the hill, greeting those he passed, and stopping again to regard the little flowers that blossomed by the wayside. At the corner of the plaza he met a young caballero who was glad to call him friend, one of the small band of men who had spent the night at Don Alejandro's hacienda.

"Ha! Don Diego, good day to you!" he cried. And then he lowered his voice and stepped nearer. "Has, by any chance, the man we call leader sent you a message?"

"Certainly not," Don Diego said. "Why should the man?"

"This Pulido business. It seems an outrage. Some of us have been wondering if our leader intends to take a hand in it. We have been anticipating a message."

"By the saints! Oh, I trust not," Don Diego said. "I could not endure an adventure of any sort tonight. I—er—my head aches, and I fear I am going to have a fever. I will have to see an apothecary about it. There are shivers up and down my spine, also. Is not that a symptom? During the siesta hour I was bothered with a pain in my left leg just above the knee. It must be the weather."

"Let us hope it is not a serious problem," laughed his friend and hurried on across the plaza.

CHAPTER 30

The Sign of the Fox

An hour after dusk that night an Indian came to one of the caballeros with word that a gentleman wished to speak to him immediately. The mysterious gentleman would be waiting along the path that ran toward the San Gabriel trail. In addition, he said to tell the caballero that there was a fox in the neighborhood.

"A fox! Zorro—fox!" the caballero thought.

He went to the spot immediately, and there he found Señor Zorro on his big horse, his face masked, the cloak wrapped around his body.

"You will pass the word, caballero," Señor Zorro said. "All men who are loyal and wish to do so, meet at midnight in the little valley beyond the hill. You know the place? Yes? I will be waiting."

Then Señor Zorro wheeled his horse and dashed away in the darkness. The caballero went back to the pueblo and passed the word to those men he knew could be depended upon to spread the word to the rest. One went to Don Diego's house, but was told by the butler that Don Diego had complained of a fever and had retired to his chamber. He had left word that he was not to be disturbed for any reason.

Near midnight the caballeros began slipping from the pueblo one at a time, each on his best horse, and each armed with sword and pistol. Each man had a mask as well.

The pueblo was in darkness, except that there were lights in the tavern. Sergeant Pedro Gonzales had returned with his men just before nightfall. They were in the tavern drinking with some of his excellency's escort.

Those in the tavern had gone down the hill from the presidio, leaving their horses there. They had no thought of an encounter with Señor Zorro this night. The fat landlord was kept busy, for the soldiers from the north had coins in their purses and were willing to spend them. Sergeant Gonzales, holding the attention of the company as usual, was explaining at length what he would do to this Señor Zorro when he next met up with him.

There were lights in the big lounging room of the presidio, too, for few of the soldiers had gone to bed. And there were lights in the house where his excellency was a guest. But the remainder of the pueblo was in darkness, and the people slept.

In the jail there was no light at all except one candle burning in the office, where a sleepy man was on guard. The jailer was in his bed. Prisoners moaned on the hard benches in the prison room. Don Carlos Pulido stood before a window, looking up at the stars. His wife and daughter huddled on a bench beside him, unable to sleep in such surroundings.

The caballeros found Señor Zorro waiting for them as he had said he would.

"Are all here?" he asked then.

"All except Don Diego Vega," one replied. "He is ill with a fever, señor."

And all the caballeros chuckled, for they had an idea the fever was caused by cowardice.

"We know what has happened to Don Carlos Pulido and his family," Señor Zorro said. "We know they are innocent of any treason. They should not have been taken to jail and thrown in with common felons and drunkards. Think of those gentle ladies in such surroundings! And only because Don Carlos has the ill will of the governor! Is it the sense of the league that something be done about this?"

"Rescue them!" a caballero said; and the others growled their approval.

"We must enter the pueblo quietly," Señor Zorro said. "There is no moon. We will not be observed if we use caution. We will approach the jail from the south. Each man will have his task to do. Some will surround the building to give warning if anyone approaches. Others will enter the jail with me and rescue the prisoners."

"It is an excellent plan," one said.

"That is but a small part of it. Don Carlos is a proud man and may refuse to be rescued. We cannot allow that. Two of you will seize him and take him from the place. Two others will escort the Doña Catalina. I will care for the señorita. Now—we have them free. And then what?"

He heard murmurs, but no distinct reply, and so he continued to outline the plan.

"All will ride to the highway just below this place," he said. "At that point we will scatter. Those who have the Doña Catalina take her to the Hacienda of Don Alejandro Vega. There she can be hidden if necessary, and the governor's soldiers will hesitate before entering and seizing her. Those who have Don Carlos will take the road to Pala. Some ten miles from this pueblo they will be met by two Indians, who will give the sign of the fox. They will take Don Carlos in charge and care for him.

"When these things are done, each caballero will ride to his home quietly and alone, using great caution. I will give the señorita into the keeping of old Friar Felipe, a man we can trust, and he will hide her. Then we will watch to see what the governor does."

"What can he do?" a caballero asked. "Search for them, of course."

"We must await developments," Señor Zorro said.

Then he named the men for each task. They left the little valley and rode slowly and cautiously around the town and approached it from the south.

They heard the soldiers shouting and singing in the tavern, saw the lights in the presidio, and crept toward the jail quietly, riding two by two.

In a short time it had been surrounded by quiet, determined men. Señor Zorro and four others dismounted and went to the door of the building.

CHAPTER 31

The Rescue

Señor Zorro knocked on the door with the hilt of his sword. They heard a man gasp inside, then heard his steps on the stone flooring. After a little time light showed through the cracks, and the small window was opened. The sleepy face of the guard appeared.

"What do you want?" he asked.

Señor Zorro thrust the muzzle of his pistol through the opening and into the man's face.

"Open, if you value your life! Open—and make not the slightest sound!" Señor Zorro commanded.

"What—what is this?"

"Señor Zorro is talking to you!"

"By the saints—"

"Open, fool, or you die instantly!"

"I—I'll open the door. Do not shoot, good Señor Zorro! I am only a poor guard and not a fighting man! I pray you do not shoot!"

"Open quickly!"

They heard him rattling the keys and then

the lock turned. The heavy door was thrown open.

Señor Zorro and his four companions rushed inside and slammed and fastened the door again. The guard found the muzzle of a pistol pressed against the side of his head. He would have knelt before these five masked and terrible men, only one of them caught him by the hair and held him up.

"Where does the keeper of this infernal hole sleep?" Señor Zorro demanded.

"In that room, señor," the guard said, pointing across the office.

"And where have you put Don Carlos Pulido and his ladies?"

"In the common prison room, señor."

Señor Zorro motioned to the others, strode across the room, and threw open the door to the jailer's chamber. The man already was sitting up in bed, having heard the sounds in the other room. He blinked in fright when he saw the highwayman.

"Do not make a move, señor," Zorro warned. "One screech, and you are a dead man."

"May the saints preserve me—"

"Where are the keys to the prison rooms?"

"On—on that table, señor."

Señor Zorro picked them up and then whirled upon the jailer again and rushed toward him.

"Lie down!" he commanded. "On your face, scoundrel!"

Señor Zorro tore strips from a blanket and tied the jailer's hands and feet and gagged him.

"To escape death," he said then, "it is necessary for you to remain exactly as you are now, without making a sound, for some time after we have left the jail. I will leave it to your own judgment to decide the length of time."

Then he hurried back into the main office, beckoned the others, and led the way down the evil-smelling hall.

"Which door?" he asked of the guard. "The second one, señor."

They hurried to it. Señor Zorro unlocked it and threw it open. He forced the guard to hold a candle high above his head.

A gasp of pity came from beneath the highwayman's mask. He saw the aged don standing by the window, saw the two women crouched on the bench, saw the vile companions they had in this miserable place.

"May Heaven forgive the governor!" he cried. Señorita Lolita looked up in alarm, and then gave a glad cry. Don Carlos whirled at the highwayman's words.

"Señor Zorro!" he gasped.

"The same, Don Carlos. I have come with some friends to rescue you."

"I cannot allow it, señor. I will not run away from what is in store for me. And it would gain me little to have you do the rescuing. I am accused now of protecting you. How will it look, then, if you help me escape?"

"There is no time for argument," Señor Zorro said. "I am not alone in this. I have twenty-six men with me. You and your family will not spend an entire night in this miserable hole if we can prevent it. Caballeros!"

The last word was one of command. Two of the caballeros threw themselves on Don Carlos, subdued him quickly, and half carried him into the hall. Two others grasped the Doña Catalina by the arms, as gently as they could, and carried her along.

Señor Zorro bowed before the señorita and extended a hand, which she clasped gladly.

"You must trust me, señorita," he said.

"To love is to trust, señor."

"Everything has been arranged. Ask no questions. Come."

He threw an arm around her and led her from the prison room, leaving the door open behind him. If some of the miserable wretches there could make their way out of the building, Señor Zorro had no wish to prevent them. More than half of them, he judged, were there because of prejudice or injustice.

Don Carlos was shouting that he refused to be rescued and that he would stay and face the governor at the trial. Doña Catalina was whimpering a bit because of fright but made no resistance.

They reached the office, and Señor Zorro ordered the guard to a corner of it, with instructions to remain there quietly for some time after they had gone. Then one of the caballeros threw open the outside door.

There was an uproar outside at that moment. Two soldiers had approached with a fellow caught stealing at the tavern, and the caballeros had stopped them. One glance at the masked faces had been enough to tell the troopers that here was something wrong.

A soldier fired a pistol, and a caballero answered the fire, neither hitting the mark. But the shooting was enough to attract the attention of those in the tavern and of the guards at the presidio.

The guards mounted and spurred down the hill to find out what caused such an uproar at that hour of the night. Sergeant Pedro Gonzales and others hurried from the tavern. Señor Zorro and his companions found themselves facing resistance when they least expected it.

The jailer had gathered courage enough to work himself free. He shrieked through a window of his chamber that prisoners were being rescued by Señor Zorro. His shriek was understood by Sergeant Gonzales, who screeched for his men to follow him.

But the caballeros had their three rescued prisoners on horseback. They spurred through the gathering throng and dashed across the plaza toward the highway.

Shots flew about them, but no man was hit. Don Carlos Pulido was still screaming that he refused to be rescued. Doña Catalina had fainted.

Señor Zorro rode wildly with the Señorita Lolita in the saddle before him. He spurred his magnificent horse ahead of all the others and led the way to the highroad. When he had reached it, he pulled up his mount and watched the others come galloping to the spot.

"Carry out your orders, caballeros!" he commanded, when he saw that there were no casualties.

The band divided into three detachments. One rushed along the Pala Road with Don Carlos. Another took the highway that would lead them to the Hacienda of Don Alejandro. Señor Zorro, riding without any of his comrades at his side, galloped toward Friar Felipe's place, the señorita's arms clasped tightly about his neck, and the señorita's voice in his ear.

"I knew that you would come for me, señor," she said. "I knew you would not see me and my parents remain in that miserable place."

Señor Zorro did not answer her with words, but his arm pressed the señorita closer to him.

He had reached the crest of the first hill, and now he stopped the horse to listen for sounds of pursuit, and to watch the flickering lights far behind.

There was a multitude of lights in the plaza now, and in all the houses, for the pueblo had been aroused. The presidio building was ablaze with light, and he could hear a trumpet being blown, and knew that every available trooper would be sent on the chase.

The sound of galloping horses came to his ears. The troopers knew which direction the rescuers had traveled. The pursuit would be swift and relentless.

But one thing pleased Señor Zorro as his horse galloped down the dusty highway and the señorita clung to him and the sharp wind cut into

CHAPTER 32

Close Quarters

Over the hills peeped the moon.

Señor Zorro would have preferred the sky heavy with clouds and the moon obscured, could he have had things his own way. As it was, he was riding along the upper trail. His pursuers were close behind and could see him against the brightening sky.

The horses ridden by the troopers were fresh, too, and those belonging to the men of his excellency's escort were able to endure many miles of travel at a terrific pace.

But now the highwayman thought only of getting all the speed possible out of his own horse. He wished to put as much distance as possible between himself and those who followed. At the end of his journey he would need quite a little time, if he was to accomplish what he had set out to do.

He bent low over the señorita, making himself almost a part of the animal he rode. He reached the crest of another hill and glanced back before he began the descent into the valley. He could see the foremost of his pursuers.

Had Señor Zorro been alone, the situation would have caused him no concern. He had often escaped from situations more difficult than this. But the señorita was on the saddle before him now, and he wanted to get her to a place of safety.

Mile after mile he rode, the señorita clinging to him, neither speaking a word. Señor Zorro knew that he had gained some on those who followed but not enough to suit his purpose.

Now he urged his horse to greater effort. They flew along the dusty highway, past haciendas where the hounds barked in sudden alarm, past the huts of Indians where the clamor of beating hoofs on the hard road caused men and women to rush to their doors.

Once he charged through a flock of sheep that were being driven to Reina de Los Angeles and the market there, and scattered them to either side of the road, leaving cursing herders behind him. The herders gathered the flock again, just in time to have the pursuing soldiers scatter it once more.

On and on he rode, until he could see, far ahead, the mission buildings at San Gabriel glistening in the moonlight. He came to a fork in the road and took the trail that ran to the right, toward the Hacienda of Friar Felipe.

Señor Zorro had known that the Señorita Lolita would have to be left either where there were women or else where there was a robed Franciscan to stand guard over her, for Señor Zorro was determined to protect his lady's good name. He was pinning his faith to old Friar Felipe.

Now the horse was galloping over softer ground and was not making such good speed. Señor Zorro had little hope that the troopers would turn into the San Gabriel Road when they arrived at the fork. Because of the moonlight, they would certainly catch sight of him.

He was within a mile of Friar Felipe's hacienda now. Once more he gave his horse the spurs in an effort to obtain greater speed.

"I will have little time, señorita," he said, bending over her and speaking into her ear. "Everything may depend upon whether I have been able to judge a man correctly. I ask only that you trust me."

"You know that I do, señor."

"And you must trust the man to whom I am carrying you, señorita, and listen well to his advice. The man is a friar."

"Then everything will be well, señor," she replied, clinging to him closely.

"If the saints are kind, we will meet again soon, señorita. I will count the hours. I believe there are happier days ahead for us."

"May Heaven grant it," the girl breathed.

"Where there is love, there is hope, señorita."

"Then my hope is great, señor."

"And mine," he said.

He turned his horse into Friar Felipe's driveway now and dashed toward the house. His intention was to stop only long enough to leave the girl, hoping that Friar Felipe would give her protection, and then ride on, making considerable noise and drawing the troopers after him. He wanted them to think that he was merely taking a short cut across Friar Felipe's land to the other road, and that he had not stopped at the house.

He reined in his horse before the veranda steps and sprang to the ground. Lifting the señorita from the saddle, he hurried with her to the door. He beat against it with his fist, praying that Friar Felipe was a light sleeper. From the far distance there came the low drumming sound of the hoofs of his pursuers' horses.

It seemed to Señor Zorro that it was an age before the old friar threw open the door and stood framed in it, holding a candle in one hand. The highwayman stepped in swiftly and closed the door behind him. Friar Felipe had taken a step backward in astonishment when he had beheld the masked man and the señorita.

"I am Señor Zorro, Friar," the highwayman said, speaking swiftly and quietly. "Perhaps you may feel that you owe me a small debt for certain things?"

"For punishing those who mistreated me, I owe you a large debt, caballero," Friar Felipe replied.

"I made no mistake in reading your character," Señor Zorro went on. "This is Señorita Lolita, the only daughter of Don Carlos Pulido."

"Ha!"

"Don Carlos is a friend of the friars, as you well know. Today the governor came to Reina de Los Angeles and had Don Carlos arrested and thrown into the jail on a charge that has no truth. He also had the Doña Catalina and this young lady put in jail, in the same prison room with drunkards and women of questionable character. With the aid of some good friends, I rescued them."

"May the saints bless you, señor, for that kind action!" Friar Felipe cried.

"Troopers are pursuing us, Friar. I ask that you take the señorita and hide her, Friar—unless you fear that such a course may cause you grave trouble."

"Señor!" Friar Felipe thundered.

"If the soldiers take her, they will put her in jail again and probably she will be mistreated. Care for her, then, protect her, and you will more than repay any obligation you may feel that you owe me."

"And you, señor?"

"I will ride on, that the troopers may pursue me and not stop here at your house. I will communicate with you later, Friar. It is agreed between us?"

"It is agreed," Friar Felipe replied solemnly.

The two men clasped their hands together briefly. Then Señor Zorro whirled toward the door.

"Blow out your candle," he directed. "They must see no light when I open the door."

In an instant they were in darkness. Señorita Lolita felt Señor Zorro's lips press against her own for a brief moment and knew that he had raised the bottom of his mask to give her this caress. Then she felt one of Friar Felipe's strong arms around her.

"Be of good courage, daughter," the friar said. "Señor Zorro, it appears, has as many lives as a cat."

The highwayman laughed lightly at that, opened the door and darted through, closing it softly behind him. And he was gone.

Great eucalyptus trees shrouded the front of the house in shadows. In the midst of these shadows was Señor Zorro's horse. He noticed, as he ran toward the beast, that the soldiers were galloping down the driveway. They were much nearer than he had expected to find them when he emerged from the house.

He ran quickly toward his mount, tripped on a stone, and fell, frightening the animal so that it darted half a dozen paces away, into the full moonlight.

The first of his pursuers shouted when he saw the horse and dashed toward it. Señor Zorro picked himself up, gave a quick spring, caught the reins from the ground, and vaulted into the saddle.

But they were upon him now, surrounding him, their blades flashing in the moonlight. He heard the harsh voice of Sergeant Gonzales ordering the men.

"Alive, if you can, soldiers! His excellency would like to see the rogue suffer for his crimes. At him, troopers! By the saints!"

Señor Zorro parried a stroke with difficulty and found himself unhorsed. On foot he fought his way back into the shadows, and the troopers charged after him. With his back to the trunk of a tree, Señor Zorro fought them off.

Three sprang from their saddles to rush in at him. He darted from the tree to another, but could not reach his horse. But one belonging to a dismounted trooper was near him, and he vaulted into the saddle and dashed down the slope toward the barns and corral.

"After the rogue!" he heard Sergeant Gonzales shouting. "His excellency will have us skinned alive if this pretty highwayman escapes us now!"

They charged after him, eager to win promotion and the reward. But Señor Zorro was far enough ahead of them to enable him to play a trick. As he came into the shadow cast by a big barn, he slipped from the saddle, at the same time giving the horse a cut with his spurs. The animal plunged ahead, snorting with pain and fright, running swiftly through the darkness toward the corral below. The soldiers dashed by in pursuit.

Señor Zorro waited until they were past and then he ran quickly up the hill again. But he saw that some of the troopers had remained behind to guard the house, so he could not reach his horse.

Once more there rang out that peculiar cry, half-shriek and half-moan, with which Señor Zorro had startled those at the Hacienda of Don Carlos Pulido. His horse raised its head, whinnied once in answer to his call, and galloped toward him.

Señor Zorro was in the saddle in an instant, spurring across a field directly in front of him. His horse went over a stone fence as if it did not exist. And after him speedily came a part of the troopers.

They charged at him from both sides, met behind him, followed, and strained to cut down his lead. He could hear Sergeant Pedro Gonzales shouting lustily.

He hoped that he had drawn them all away from Friar Felipe's house but he was not sure.

The thing that demanded his attention the most now was his own escape.

He urged his horse cruelly, knowing that this journey across plowed ground was taking the animal's strength. He longed for a hard trail, the broad highway.

And finally he reached the highway. Now he turned his horse's head toward Reina de Los Angeles, for he had work to do there. There was no señorita before him on the saddle now and the horse felt the difference.

Señor Zorro glanced behind and saw he was outrunning the soldiers. Over the next hill and he would be able to elude them!

But he had to be on guard, of course, for there might be troopers in front of him, too. His excellency might have sent reinforcements to Sergeant Gonzales, or might have men watching from the tops of the hills.

He glanced at the sky and saw that the moon was about to disappear behind a bank of clouds. He would have to make use of the short period of darkness, he knew.

Down into the little valley he rode and looked back to find that his pursuers were only at the crest of the hill. Then came the darkness and at the proper time. Señor Zorro had a lead of half a mile on the pursuing soldiers now, but it was not his intention to allow them to chase him into the pueblo.

He had friends in this locality. Beside the highway was an adobe hut, where there lived an Indian Señor Zorro had saved from a beating. He dismounted before the hut and kicked against the door. The frightened Indian opened it.

"I am pursued," Señor Zorro said.

That appeared to be all that was necessary, for the man immediately threw the door of the hut open wider. Señor Zorro led his horse inside, almost filling the tiny building, and the door was hastily shut again.

Behind it, the highwayman and the Indian stood listening.

CHAPTER 33

Flight and Pursuit

That the pursuit of Señor Zorro from the jail had been taken up so quickly was due to Sergeant Pedro Gonzales.

Sergeant Gonzales had heard the shots and had rushed from the tavern with the other troopers at his heels, glad of an excuse to escape without paying for the wine he had ordered. He had heard the shout of the jailer and immediately had grasped the situation.

"Señor Zorro is rescuing the prisoners!" he screeched. "The highwayman is in our midst again! After him! There is a reward—"

They knew all about the reward. They rushed for their horses, swung themselves into their saddles, and dashed across the plaza toward the jail with Sergeant Gonzales at their head.

They saw the gang of masked caballeros galloping across the plaza. Sergeant Gonzales rubbed his eyes with the back of one hand and swore softly that he had been taking too much wine. He had lied so often about Señor Zorro having a band of men, that here was the band materialized out of his falsehoods.

When the caballeros split into three detachments, Sergeant Gonzales and his troopers were so near them that they observed the maneuver. Gonzales quickly made three troops of the men who followed him and sent a troop after each band.

He saw the leader of the caballeros turn toward San Gabriel, and he recognized the horse the highwayman rode. He took after Señor Zorro, more interested in capturing or killing the highwayman than in retaking the rescued prisoners. Sergeant Pedro Gonzales had not forgotten the rainy night that Señor Zorro had made a fool of him in the tavern.

He had seen Señor Zorro's horse run before, and he was surprised now because the highwayman was not putting greater distance between himself and his pursuers. And Sergeant Gonzales guessed the reason—that Señor Zorro had Señorita Lolita Pulido on the saddle before him.

Gonzales was in the lead. Now and then he turned his head and shouted orders and encouragement to his troopers. The miles flew beneath them, and Gonzales was glad that he was keeping Señor Zorro in sight.

"To Friar Felipe's—that is where he is riding!" Gonzales told himself. "I knew that old friar was working with the bandit! He tricked me when I searched for Señor Zorro at his hacienda before. Perhaps this highwayman has a clever hiding place there. Ha! By the saints, I will not be fooled again!"

On they rode, now and then catching glimpses of the man they pursued, and always in the minds of Gonzales and his troopers were thoughts of the reward and promotion. Their horses were beginning to tire a bit, but they did not spare the animals.

They saw Señor Zorro turn into the driveway that led to Friar Felipe's house. Sergeant Gonzales chuckled low down in his throat for guessing correctly.

He had the highwayman now! If Señor Zorro continued to ride, he could be seen and followed because of the bright moonlight. If he stopped, Señor Zorro could not hope to cope successfully with a dozen troopers lead by Gonzales.

They dashed up to the front of the house and started to surround it. They saw Señor Zorro's horse. And then they saw the highwayman himself. Gonzales cursed because half a dozen troopers were between him and his prey, and were at him with their swords, threatening to end the business before Gonzales could reach the scene.

He tried to force his horse into the fight. He saw Señor Zorro spring into a saddle and dash away, and the troopers after him. Gonzales, not

being close, ordered some of his soldiers surround the house so that none could leave it.

Then he saw Señor Zorro take the stone
fence, and started in pursuit, all except the guards
around the house joining him. But Sergeant
Gonzales went only as far as the crest of the first
hill. He noticed how the highwayman's horse
was running and realized that he could not be
overtaken. Perhaps the sergeant could gain some
glory if he returned to Friar Felipe's house and
recaptured the señorita.

When he dismounted in front of the house,
his men reported that no one had attempted to
leave the building. He called two of his men to
his side and knocked on the door. Almost
instantly it was opened by Friar Felipe.

"I see you just happen to be out of bed,
Friar," Gonzales said. "Did our noise wake you?"

"I heard sounds of combat—"

"And you may hear more, Friar, else feel the
sting of a whip again, unless you answer questions quickly. Do you deny that Señor Zorro has
been here?"

"I do not."

"Ha! Now we have it. You admit, then, that
you are secretly working with this pretty highwayman, that you hide him sometimes? You
admit that, Friar?"

"I admit nothing of the sort," Friar Felipe
replied. "I never set eyes on this Señor Zorro, to

my knowledge, until a few minutes ago."

"That is a likely story. What did this Señor Zorro wish?"

"You were so close upon the man's heels, señor, that he scarce had time to wish for anything," Friar Felipe said.

"Yet you spoke with him?"

"I opened the door at his knock, señor, the same as I opened it at yours."

"What did he say?"

"That soldiers were pursuing him."

"And he asked that you hide him, so he could escape capture at our hands?"

"He did not."

"Wanted a fresh horse, did he?"

"He did not say so, señor. If he is such a thief as people say, he would merely have taken a horse without asking, had he wanted it."

"Ha! What business did he have with you, then? It would be wise for you to answer openly, Friar."

"Did I say that he had business with me?"

"Ha! By the saints—"

"The saints are better off your lips, señor— boaster and drunkard!"

"Do you wish to receive another beating, Friar? I am riding on his excellency's business. Do not you delay me further! What did this pretty highwayman say?"

"Nothing that I am at liberty to repeat to

you, señor," Friar Felipe said.

Sergeant Gonzales pushed him aside roughly and entered the living room. His two troopers followed at his heels.

"Light the candles," Gonzales commanded his men. "We will search the house."

"You search my poor house?" Friar Felipe cried. "And what do you expect to find?"

"I expect to find the piece of merchandise Señor Zorro left here, Friar."

"What do you imagine he left?"

"Ha! A package of clothing, I suppose! A bundle of loot! A bottle of wine! A saddle to be mended! What would the fellow leave, Friar? One thing impresses me—Señor Zorro's horse carried double when he arrived at your house and was carrying none but Señor Zorro when he departed."

"And you expect to find—"

"The second rider," replied Gonzales. "If we do not find it, we may try a twist or two of your arm to see whether you can be made to speak."

"You would dare? You would so insult a friar? You would descend to torture?"

"Meal mush and goat's milk!" said Sergeant Gonzales. "You fooled me once in some manner, but you will not fool me again. Search the house, troopers."

"There may come a day when persecution will cease," Friar Felipe thundered. "When this disorder ends and honest men be given their just dues! When honest men no longer have the fruits of their labor stolen by dishonest politicians!"

"Goat's milk and meal mush, Friar*!*"

"When there will be a thousand Señor Zorros, and more if necessary, to ride up and down El Camino Real and punish those who do wrong! Sometimes I wish that I were not a friar, that I might play such a game myself!"

"Ha! Now you grow angry, and that is against your principles."

"You have about as much knowledge of a Franciscan's principles as has the horse you ride."

"I ride a wise horse, a noble animal. He comes when I call and gallops when I command. Do not deride him until you ride him. Ha! An excellent jest."

"Imbecile!"

"Meal mush and goat's milk!" said Sergeant Gonzales.

CHAPTER 34

The Blood of the Pulidos

The two troopers came back into the room. They had searched every corner of the house, they reported, and no trace had been found of any person other than Friar Felipe's servants.

"Ha! Hidden away well, no doubt!" Gonzales said. "Friar, what is that in the corner of the room?"

"Bales of hides," Friar Felipe replied.

"I have been noticing it from time to time. The dealer from San Gabriel said the hides he purchased of you were not properly cured. Are those?"

"I think you will find them so."

"Then why did they move?" Sergeant Gonzales asked. "Three times I saw the corner of a bale move. Soldiers, search there."

Friar Felipe sprang to his feet.

"Enough of this nonsense," he cried. "You have searched and found nothing. Search the barns next and then go! At least let me be master in my own house. You have disturbed my rest enough as it is."

"You will take a solemn oath, Friar, that there is nothing alive behind those bales of hides?"

Friar Felipe hesitated, and Sergeant Gonzales grinned.

"Not ready to swear falsely, eh?" the sergeant asked. "I had a thought you would hesitate at that, my robed Franciscan. Soldiers, search the bales."

The two men started toward the corner. But they had not covered one half the distance when Señorita Lolita Pulido stood up behind the bales of hides and faced them.

"Ha! Unearthed at last!" Gonzales cried. "Here is the package Señor Zorro left in the friar's keeping! And a pretty package it is! Back to jail she goes, and this escape will but make her final sentence more harsh!"

But there was Pulido blood in the señorita's veins, and Gonzales had not taken that into account. Now the señorita stepped to the end of the pile of hides, so that light from the candles struck full upon her.

"One moment, señores," she said.

One hand came from behind her back. In it she held a long, keen knife such as sheep skinners used. She put the point of the knife against her breast and regarded them bravely.

"Señorita Lolita Pulido does not return to the foul jail now or at any time, señores," she said. "Rather would she plunge this knife into her heart, and so die as a woman of good blood should. If his excellency wishes for a dead prisoner, he may have one."

Sergeant Gonzales uttered an exclamation of annoyance. He did not doubt that the señorita would do as she had threatened if the men made an attempt to seize her. And while he might have ordered the attempt in the case of an ordinary prisoner, he was not sure that the governor would say he had done right if he ordered it now. After all, Señorita Pulido was the daughter of a don, and her self-inflicted death might cause trouble for his excellency. It might prove the spark to the powder keg.

"Señorita, the person who takes his or her own life risks eternal damnation," the sergeant said. "Ask this friar if it is not so. You are only under arrest, not convicted and sentenced. If you are innocent, no doubt you soon will be set at liberty."

"It is no time for lying speeches, señor," the girl replied. "I realize the circumstances only too well, I have said that I will not return to jail, and I mean it. One step toward me and I take my own life."

"Señorita—" Friar Felipe began.

"It is useless to attempt to prevent me, good Friar," she interrupted. "I have pride left me, thank the saints. His excellency gets only my dead body, if he gets me at all."

"Here is a pretty mess," Sergeant Gonzales exclaimed. "I suppose there is nothing for us to do except give the señorita to her freedom."

"Ah, no, señor!" she cried quickly. "You are clever, but not clever enough by far. You would continue to have your men surround the house. You would watch for an opportunity, and then seize me."

Gonzales growled low in his throat, for that had been his intention, and the girl had read it.

"You will stay here," she said. "Walk backward and stand against the wall, señores. Do it immediately, or I plunge this knife into my breast."

They could do nothing except obey. The soldiers looked to the sergeant for instructions. The sergeant was afraid to risk the señorita's death, knowing it would call down on his head the wrath of the governor.

Perhaps, after all, it would be better to let the girl leave the house. She could be captured later.

She watched them closely as she darted across the room to the door. The knife was still held at her breast.

"Friar Felipe, do you wish to go with me?" she asked. "You may be punished if you remain."

"But I must remain, señorita. I could not run away. May the saints protect you!"

She faced Gonzales and the soldiers once more.

"I am going through this door," she said. "You will remain in this room. There are troopers outside, of course, and they will try to stop me. I will tell them that I have your permission to leave. If they call and ask you, you are to say that it is so."

"And if I do not?"

"Then I use the knife, señor."

She opened the door, turned her head for an instant, and glanced out.

"I trust that your horse is an excellent one, señor, for I intend to use it," she told the sergeant.

She darted suddenly through the door and slammed it shut behind her.

"After her!" Gonzales cried. "I looked into her eyes! She will not use the knife—she fears it!"

He hurled himself across the room, the two soldiers with him. But Friar Felipe had been passive long enough. He went into action now. He did not stop to consider the consequences. He threw out one leg and tripped Sergeant Gonzales. The two troopers crashed into him, and all went to the floor in a tangle.

Friar Felipe had gained some time for her, and it had been enough. The señorita had rushed to the horse and jumped into the saddle. Her tiny feet did not reach halfway to the sergeant's stirrups, but she thought nothing of that.

She wheeled the horse's head, kicked at his

sides as a trooper rushed around the corner of the house. A pistol ball whistled past her head. She bent lower over the horse's neck and rode.

Now a cursing Sergeant Gonzales was on the veranda, shouting for his men to follow her. The moon was behind a bank of clouds again. They could not tell the direction the señorita was taking except by listening for the sounds of the horse's hoofs. But they had to stop to do that— and if they stopped they lost time and distance.

CHAPTER 35

The Clash of Blades Again

Señor Zorro stood like a statue in the Indian's hut, one hand grasping his horse's muzzle. The Indian crouched at his side.

Down the highway came the drumming of horses' hoofs. Then the pursuit swept by, the men calling to one another and cursing the darkness. The sounds disappeared down the valley.

Señor Zorro opened the door and glanced out, listened for a moment, and then led out his horse.

"You have done me a great service," he said.

"You owe me nothing, señor," the Indian said.

Señor Zorro vaulted into the saddle and turned his horse up the steep slope of the hill behind the hut. The animal made little noise as it climbed to the summit. Señor Zorro descended into the depression on the other side and came to a narrow trail. He rode along this at a slow gallop, stopping now and then to listen for sounds of other horsemen.

He rode toward Reina de Los Angeles, but he appeared to be in no hurry. Señor Zorro had another adventure planned for this night, and it had to be accomplished at a certain time and under certain conditions.

It was two hours later when he came to the crest of the hill above the town. He sat quietly in the saddle for some time, looking down on the scene. Now and then he could make out the plaza as the moonlight came and went.

He saw no troopers, heard nothing of them. He decided that none had yet returned from the pursuit. In the tavern there were lights, and in the presidio and in the house where his excellency was a guest.

Señor Zorro waited until it was dark and then urged his horse forward slowly, but off the main highway. He circled the pueblo and approached the presidio from the rear.

He dismounted and led his horse, going forward slowly, often stopping to listen, for this was a very ticklish business. A mistake now could mean disaster.

He stopped the horse behind the presidio where the wall of the building would cast a shadow if the moon came from behind the clouds again. He went forward cautiously, following the wall as he had done on that other night.

When he came to the office window, he peered inside. Captain Ramón was there alone, looking over some reports spread on the table before him, evidently awaiting the return of his men.

Señor Zorro crept to the corner of the building and found there was no guard. He had guessed that the commandant had sent every available man to the chase. But he knew that he would have to act quickly, for some of the troopers might return.

He slipped through the door and crossed the big lounging room, and came to the door of the office. His pistol was in his hand. Beneath the mask, Señor Zorro's lips were crushed in a thin, straight line of determination.

As on that other night, Captain Ramón whirled around in his chair when he heard the door open behind him, and once more he saw the eyes of Señor Zorro glittering through his mask, saw the muzzle of the pistol menacing him.

"Not a move. Not a sound. It would give me pleasure to fill your body with hot lead," Señor Zorro said. "You are alone—your silly troopers are chasing me where I am not."

"By the saints—" Captain Ramón breathed.

"Not so much as a whisper, señor, if you hope to live. Turn your back to me."

"You would murder me?"

"I am not that sort, commandant. And I said for you to make not a sound. Put your hands behind your back, for I am going to bind your wrists."

Captain Ramón complied. Señor Zorro stepped forward swiftly and bound the wrists with his own sash, which he tore from his waist. Then he whirled Captain Ramón around so that he faced him.

"We are going to call upon the governor."

"To call—"

"Upon his excellency, I said. And do not speak again. Come with me."

He grasped Captain Ramón by the arm and hurried him from the office, across the lounging room, out of the door. He directed him around the building to where the horse was waiting.

"Mount!" he commanded. "I will sit behind you, with the muzzle of this pistol at the base of your brain. Make no mistake, commandant, unless you are tired of life. I am a determined man this night."

Captain Ramón mounted as he was directed, and the highwayman mounted behind him, holding the reins with one hand and the pistol with the other. Captain Ramón could feel the touch of cold steel at the back of his head.

Señor Zorro guided his horse with his knees instead of with the reins. He urged the beast down the slope and circled the town once more, keeping away from the beaten trails, and so approached the rear of the house where his excellency was a guest.

Here was the difficult part of the adventure.

He forced the captain to dismount and led him to the rear wall of the house. There was a patio there, and they entered it.

It appeared that Señor Zorro knew the interior of the house well. He entered it through a servant's room, taking Captain Ramón with him, and passed through into a hall without awakening the sleeping servant. They went along the hall slowly. From one room came the sound of snoring. From beneath the door of another light streamed.

Señor Zorro stopped before that door and looked through a crack at the side of it. If Captain Ramón had any thoughts of calling for help, the touch of the pistol at the back of his head caused him to forget them.

And he had little time to think of a way out of this predicament, for suddenly Señor Zorro threw open the door, hurled Captain Ramón through it, followed himself, and shut the door quickly behind him. In the room there were his excellency and his host.

"Silence, and do not move," Señor Zorro said. "The slightest alarm, and I put a pistol ball through the governor's head. That is understood?"

"Señor Zorro!" the governor gasped.

"The same, your excellency. I ask your host to be not frightened, for I mean him no harm if he sits quietly until I am done. Captain Ramón, kindly sit across the table from the governor. I am delighted to find the head of the state awake and awaiting news from those who are chasing me. His brain will be clear, and he can understand better what is said."

"What is the meaning of this outrage?" the governor exclaimed. "Captain Ramón, seize this man! You are an officer—"

"Do not blame the commandant," Señor Zorro said. "He knows it is death to make a move. There is a little matter that needs explanation, and since I cannot come to you in broad day, as a man should, I am forced to adopt this method. Make yourselves comfortable, señores. This may take a little time."

His excellency fidgeted in his chair.

"You have insulted a family of good blood, your excellency," Señor Zorro went on. "You have ordered thrown into your miserable jail a respected gentleman and his gentle wife and innocent daughter."

"They are traitors," his excellency said.

"What act of treason have they committed?"

"You are an outlaw with a price put on your head. They have been guilty of protecting you, giving you aid."

"Where did you get this information?"

"Captain Ramón has much evidence."

"Ha! The commandant, eh? We will see about that! Captain Ramón is present, and we can get at the truth. May I ask the nature of your evidence?"

"You were at the Pulido hacienda," the governor said.

"I admit it."

"A servant saw you and carried word to the presidio. The soldiers hurried out to capture you."

"A moment. Who said a servant sounded the alarm?"

"Captain Ramón assured me so."

"Here is the first chance for the captain to speak the truth. As a matter of fact, commandant, was it not Don Carlos Pulido himself who sent the servant? The truth!"

"It was a servant brought word."

"And he did not tell your sergeant that Don Carlos had sent him? Did he not say that Don Carlos had slipped him the information in whispers while he was carrying his fainting wife to her room? Is it not true that Don Carlos did his best to hold me at his hacienda until the soldiers arrived, that I might be captured? Did not Don Carlos try to show his loyalty to the governor?"

"By the saints, Ramón, you never told me this!" his excellency cried.

"They are traitors," the captain declared stubbornly.

"What other evidence?" Señor Zorro asked.

"Why, when the soldiers arrived, you concealed yourself by some trick," the governor said. "And after Captain Ramón arrived, you crept from a closet, ran him through treacherously from behind, and made your escape. It is clear that Don Carlos had hidden you in the closet."

"By the saints!" Señor Zorro swore. "I had thought, Captain Ramón, that you were man enough to admit defeat. Tell the truth!"

"That is—the truth."

"Tell the truth!" Señor Zorro commanded, stepping closer to him and bringing up the pistol. "I came from that closet and spoke to you. I gave you time to draw blade and get on guard. We fenced for fully ten minutes, did we not? When I could have slain you easily, I but scratched your shoulder. Is not that the truth? Answer, if you hope to live!"

Captain Ramón licked his dry lips and could not meet the governor's eyes.

"Answer!" Señor Zorro thundered.

"It is—the truth," the captain acknowledged.

"Ha! So I ran you through from behind, eh? It is an insult to my blade to have it enter your body. You see, your excellency, what manner of man you have for commandant here. Is there more evidence?"

"There is," the governor said. "When the Pulidos were guests at the house of Don Diego Vega, and Don Diego was away, Captain Ramón went to pay his respects and found you there alone with the señorita."

"And that shows what?"

"That you are working secretly with the Pulidos. That they protected you even in the house of Don Diego, a loyal man. And when the captain discovered you there, the señorita flung herself upon him and held him—delayed him, rather—until you made your escape through a window. Is not that enough?"

Señor Zorro bent forward, and his eyes seemed to burn through the mask and into those of Captain Ramón.

"So that is the tale he told, eh?" the highwayman said. "As a matter of fact, Captain Ramón went to the house, found her alone, and forced himself on her. He even told her that she should not object, since her father was in the bad graces of the governor. He attempted to kiss her, and she called for help. I responded."

"How did you happen to be there?"

"I do not care to answer that, but I take my oath the señorita did not know of my presence. She called for aid, and I responded. I made this thing you call a commandant kneel before her and apologize. And then I took him to the door and kicked him out into the dust! And afterward I visited him at the presidio and told him that he had insulted a noble señorita—"

"It appears that you hold some love for her yourself," the governor said.

"I do, your excellency, and am proud to admit it."

"Ha! You condemn her and her parents by that statement! Do you deny now they are helping you?"

"I do. Her parents do not know of our love."

"This señorita sounds rather unusual."

"Señor! Governor or no, I must insist that you show the proper respect for her," Señor Zorro cried. "I have told you what happened that night at the house of Don Diego Vega. Captain Ramón will testify that what I have said is the exact truth. Is it not, commandant? Answer!"

"It—it is the truth." The captain gulped, looking at the muzzle of the highwayman's pistol.

"Then you have told me falsehood, and can no longer be an officer of mine!" the governor cried. "This highwayman can do as he pleases with you. Ha! But I still believe that Don Carlos Pulido and his family are traitors. This little scene has gained you nothing, Señor Zorro. My soldiers will continue to pursue them—and you! And before they are done, I'll have the Pulidos dragged in the dirt, and I'll have you stretching a rope with your carcass!"

"Quite a bold speech," observed Señor Zorro. "Have you forgotten that your three prisoners have escaped?"

"They will be retaken."

"Time alone will tell that. And now I have

another duty to perform here. Your excellency, you will take your chair to that far corner and sit there, and your host will sit beside you. You will remain there until I have finished."

"What are you going to do?"

"Obey me," Señor Zorro cried. "I have little time for argument, even with a governor."

He watched while the two chairs were placed and the governor and his host had seated themselves. Then he stepped nearer Captain Ramón.

"You insulted an innocent young woman, commandant," he said. "For that, you will fight. Your scratched shoulder is healed now. Such a man as you is not fit to breathe God's pure air. The country is better for your absence. On your feet, señor, and on guard!"

Captain Ramón was white with rage. He knew that he was ruined. He had been forced to confess that he had lied. He had heard the governor remove his rank. And this man had been the cause of all of it.

Perhaps in his anger he could kill this Señor Zorro, stretch this Curse of Capistrano on the floor with his life blood flowing away. Perhaps, if he did that, his excellency would change his mind.

He sprang from his chair and backward to the side of the governor.

"Unfasten my wrists!" he cried. "Let me at this dog!"

"You were as good as dead before—you certainly are dead after using that word," Señor Zorro said calmly. The commandant's wrists were untied. He whipped out his blade, sprang forward with a cry, and launched a furious attack on the highwayman.

Señor Zorro gave ground, and so moved to a position where the light from the candleholder did not bother his eyes. He knew the danger in the attack of an angered man who did not fence according to the rules. And he knew, too, that such anger is spent quickly. And so he retreated step by step, guarding well, parrying vicious strokes, alert for an unexpected move.

"Run him through, Ramón, and I reinstate and promote you!" his excellency cried.

The commandant began to fight more calmly. Señor Zorro found his opponent fighting much better than he had before in Don Carlos Pulido's house at the hacienda. He was forced to fight out of a dangerous corner. The pistol he held in his left hand to intimidate the governor and his host bothered him.

Suddenly he tossed it to the table. Then he swung around so that neither of the two men could dart from a corner without risk of getting a blade between the ribs. And there he stood his ground and fought.

Captain Ramón could not force him to give way now. The highwayman's blade darted in and out, trying to find a resting place in the captain's body. Señor Zorro was eager to have an end of this and be gone. The dawn was not far away, and he feared that some trooper might come to the house with a report for the governor.

"Fight, you coward!" he cried. "Death stares you in the face! Soon it will claim you! Ha! I almost had you then! Fight, cur!"

Captain Ramón cursed and charged, but Señor Zorro drove him back. The perspiration was standing out on the captain's forehead. His breath was coming heavily from between his parted lips. His eyes were bright and bulging.

"Fight, weakling!" The highwayman taunted him. "This time I am not attacking from behind. If you have prayers to say, say them—your time grows short."

The ringing blades, the shifting feet on the floor, the heavy breathing of the combatants in this life-and-death struggle were the only sounds in the room. His excellency sat far forward on his chair, his hands gripping the edges of it so that his knuckles were white.

"Kill me this highwayman!" he shrieked. "Use your good skill, Ramón! At him!"

Captain Ramón rushed again, calling into play his last bit of strength, fencing with what skill he could command. His arms were like lead; his breath was fast. He thrust, he lunged—and made a mistake of a fraction of an inch.

Like the tongue of a serpent, Señor Zorro's blade shot in. Three times it darted forward, and on the forehead of Ramón, just above the eyes, there flamed suddenly a red, bloody letter Z.

"The Mark of Zorro!" the highwayman cried. "You wear it forever now, commandant!"

Señor Zorro's face became more stern. His blade shot in again and came out dripping red. The commandant gasped and slipped to the floor.

"You have killed him!" the governor cried. "You have taken his life, wretch!"

"Ha! I trust so. The thrust was through the heart, excellency. He never will insult a señorita again."

Señor Zorro looked down at his fallen foe, looked at the governor a moment, then wiped his blade on the sash that had bound the commandant's wrists. He returned the blade to its scabbard and picked up his pistol from the table.

"My night's work is done," he said.

"And you will hang for it!" his excellency cried.

"Perhaps—when you catch me," replied the Curse of Capistrano, bowing ceremoniously.

Then, without glancing again at the twitching body of Captain Ramón, he whirled through the door and was in the hall and rushed through it to the patio and to his horse.

CHAPTER 36

All Against Them

And he rushed into danger.

The dawn had come. The first pink streaks had appeared in the eastern sky, and then the sun had risen quickly above the hills to the east, and now the plaza was bathed in brilliance. There was no mist, no fog in the hills even. Objects on the hillsides far away stood out in relief. It was no morning in which to ride for freedom.

Señor Zorro had delayed too long with the governor and commandant. He swung into his saddle and urged his beast out of the patio—and then a full realization of his peril came to him.

Down the trail from San Gabriel came Sergeant Pedro Gonzales and his troopers. Down the Pala road came another detachment of soldiers that had been trailing the caballeros and Don Carlos. Over the hill toward the presidio came the third body of men, who had tried to recapture the Doña Catalina. Señor Zorro was hemmed in by his foes.

The Curse of Capistrano deliberately stopped his horse and for a moment considered the situation. He glanced at the three bodies of troopers, estimated the distance. And in that instant one with Sergeant Gonzales's detachment saw him and raised the alarm.

They knew that magnificent horse, that long purple cloak, that black mask and wide sombrero. They saw before them the man they had been pursuing throughout the night, the man who had made fools of them. They feared the rage of his excellency and their superior officers. In their hearts and minds was determination to capture or slay this Curse of Capistrano now as this last chance was offered them.

Señor Zorro spurred his horse and dashed across the plaza. Just as he did that, the governor and his host rushed from the house, shrieking that Señor Zorro was a murderer and should be taken. Servants in the plaza scurried for shelter; men of rank stood still and gaped in astonishment.

Señor Zorro, having crossed the plaza, drove his horse straight toward the highway. Sergeant Gonzales and his troopers rushed to cut him off, shrieking at one another, pistols in their hands, blades loosened in their scabbards.

Señor Zorro was forced to swerve from his first course, for he saw that he could not get through. He cut across the plaza again, almost running down several men of rank who were in the way. He passed within a few paces of the infuriated governor and his host, darted between two houses, and rushed toward the hills in that direction.

It appeared that he had some small chance of escaping his foes now. He cut across the open ground. From both sides the troopers galloped to meet him, flying toward the angle of the wedge, hoping to reach it in time and turn him back once more.

Gonzales was shouting orders in his great voice, and he was sending some of his men down into the pueblo so they would be in position in case the highwayman turned back again.

He reached the highway and started down it toward the south. It was not the direction he would have preferred, but he had no choice now. He dashed around a curve in the road, where some huts cut off the view—and suddenly he pulled up his horse, almost unseating himself.

For here a new menace presented itself. Straight at him along the highway flew a horse and rider, and close behind came half a dozen troopers in pursuit.

Señor Zorro whirled his horse. He could not turn to the right because of a stone fence. His horse could have jumped it, but on the other side was soft plowed ground, and he knew he could make no progress across it, and that the troopers could cut him down with a pistol bullet.

Nor could he turn to the left, for there was a sheer cliff down which he could not hope to ride with safety. He had to turn back toward Sergeant

Gonzales and the men who rode with him, hoping to get a distance of a couple of hundred yards, where he could make a descent, before Gonzales and his men arrived at the spot.

He gripped his sword and was prepared for fight, for he knew it was going to be close work. He glanced back over his shoulder—and gasped his surprise.

It was Señorita Lolita Pulido who rode that horse and was pursued by the half-dozen troopers. He had thought her safe at the Hacienda of Friar Felipe. Her long black hair was down and streaming out behind her. Her tiny heels were glued to the horse's flanks. She bent forward as she rode, holding the reins low down, and Señor Zorro, even in that instant, marveled at her skill.

"Señor!" he heard her shout.

And then she had reached his side, and they rode together, dashing down upon Gonzales and his troopers.

"They have been chasing me—for hours!" she gasped. "I escaped them—at Friar Felipe's!"

"Ride close! Do not waste breath!" he screeched.

"My horse—is almost done—señor!"

Señor Zorro glanced aside at the beast, and saw that it was exhausted. But there was no time to consider that now. The soldiers behind had gained some; those in front presented another menace.

Down the trail they flew, side by side, straight

at Gonzales and his men. Señor Zorro could see that pistols were out.

Now he spurred a few paces in advance of the señorita, and called to her to ride his horse's tracks. He dropped the reins on his mount's neck, and held his blade ready. He had two weapons—his blade and his horse.

Then came the crash. Señor Zorro swerved his horse at the proper instant, and the señorita followed him. He cut at the trooper on his left, swung over and cut at the one on his right. His horse crashed into that of a third trooper and hurled it against the animal the sergeant rode.

He heard shrill cries about him. He knew that the men who had been pursuing Señorita Lolita had run into the others. He knew that, in the confusion, the troopers could not use blades for fear of cutting down one another.

And then he was through them, with the señorita riding at his side again. Once more he was at the edge of the plaza. His horse was showing signs of weariness, and he had gained nothing.

The way to San Gabriel was not open. The way to Pala was closed. He could not hope to escape by cutting across soft ground. And on the opposite side of the plaza were more troopers, waiting to cut him off, no matter in which direction he started.

"We are caught!" he shouted. "But we are not done, señorita!"

"My horse is stumbling!" she cried.

Señor Zorro saw that it was so. He knew that the beast could not make another hundred yards.

"To the tavern!" he cried.

They galloped straight across the plaza. At the door of the tavern the señorita's horse staggered and fell. Señor Zorro caught the girl in his arms in time to save her from a hard fall and, still carrying her, darted through the tavern door.

"Out!" he cried to the landlord. "Out!" he shrieked to half a dozen loiterers, exhibiting his pistol. They rushed through the door and into the plaza.

The highwayman threw the door shut and bolted it. He saw that all the windows were closed with boards in place over them, except the one facing the plaza. He stepped to the table and then whirled to face the señorita.

"It may be the end," he said.

"Señor! Surely the saints will be kind to us."

"We are surrounded by foes, señorita. I do not care if I die fighting as a caballero should. But you, señorita—"

"They will never put me in the foul jail again, señor! I swear it! Rather would I die with you."

She pulled out the sheep skinner's knife, and he caught a glance of it.

"Not that, señorita!" he cried.

"I have given you my heart, señor. Either we live together or we die together."

CHAPTER 37

The Fox at Bay

He darted to the window and glanced out. The troopers were surrounding the building. He could see the governor stalking across the plaza, calling out orders. Down the San Gabriel trail came the proud Don Alejandro Vega, to pay his visit to the governor. He stopped at the plaza's edge and began questioning men regarding the cause for the commotion.

"I wonder where my brave caballeros are, those who rode with me?" Señor Zorro said, laughing.

"You expect their aid?" she asked.

"No, señorita. They would have to stand together and face the governor, tell him their intentions. It was a lark with them, and I doubt whether they take it seriously enough to stand by me now. It is not to be expected. I fight it out alone."

"Not alone, señor, when I am by your side." He clasped her in his arms, pressed her to him.

"It would be foolish for you to let my disaster

influence your life," he said. "You have never even seen my face, señorita. You could forget me. You could walk from this place and surrender, send word to Don Diego Vega that you will become his bride. The governor then would be forced to release you and clear your parents of all blame."

"Ah, señor—"

"Think, señorita. Think what it would mean. His excellency would not dare stand an instant against a Vega. Your parents would have their lands restored. You would be the bride of the richest young man in the country. You would have everything to make you happy—"

"Everything except love, señor, and without love, the rest is as nothing."

"Think, señorita, and decide for once and all. You have but a moment now!"

"I made my decision long ago, señor. A Pulido loves but once, and does not wed where she cannot love."

He pressed her close again.

Now there came a battering at the door.

"Señor Zorro!" Sergeant Gonzales cried.

"Well, señor?" Zorro asked.

"I have an offer for you from his excellency the governor."

"I am listening, loud one."

"His excellency has no wish to cause your death or injury to the señorita with you. He asks that you open the door and come out with the lady."

"And if I do?" Señor Zorro asked.

"You will be given a fair trial, and the señorita also. You may escape death and receive imprisonment instead."

"Ha! I have seen samples of his excellency's fair trials," Señor Zorro responded. "Do you think I am an imbecile?"

"His excellency says that this is the last chance, that the offer will not be renewed."

"His excellency is wise not to waste breath renewing it. He grows fat, and his breath is short."

"What can you expect to gain by resistance, save death?" Gonzales asked. "How can you hope to hold off thirty of us?"

"It has been done before, loud one."

"We can batter in the door and take you."

"After a few of you have been stretched lifeless on the floor," Señor Zorro observed. "Who will be the first through the door, my sergeant?"

"For the last time—"

"Come in and drink a mug of wine with me," said the highwayman, laughing.

"Meal mush and goat's milk!" swore Sergeant Gonzales.

There was quiet then for a time. Señor Zorro, glancing through the window cautiously, so as not to attract a pistol shot, observed that the governor was in consultation with the sergeant.

The consultation ended, and Señor Zorro darted back from the window. Almost immediately, the attack upon the door began. They were pounding at it with heavy timbers, trying to smash it down. Señor Zorro, standing in the middle of the room, pointed his pistol at the door and fired. The ball tore through the wood and somebody outside gave a shriek of pain. He darted to the table and started loading the pistol again.

Then he hurried across to the door and observed the hole where the bullet had gone through. The plank had been split, and there was quite a crack in it. Señor Zorro put the point of his blade at this crack and waited.

Again the heavy timber crashed against the door, and some trooper threw his weight against it, also. Señor Zorro's blade darted through the crack like a streak of lightning, and came back red, and again there was a shriek outside. Now a volley of pistol balls came through the door, but Señor Zorro, laughing, had sprung out of harm's way.

"Well done, señor!" Señorita Lolita cried.

"We will stamp our mark on several of these hounds before we are done," he replied.

"I wish that I could help you, señor."

"You are doing it, señorita. Your love gives me my strength."

"At the end, señor, if there is no hope—may I then see your dear face?"

"I swear it, señorita, and feel my arms about you, and my lips on yours. Death will not be so bitter then."

The attack on the door was renewed. Now pistol shots were coming through it regularly, and through the one open window also. There was nothing for Señor Zorro to do except stand in the middle of the room and wait, his blade held ready. There would be a lively few minutes, he promised, when the door was down and they rushed in at him.

It seemed to be giving way now. The señorita crept close to him, tears streaming down her cheeks, and grasped him by the arm.

"Just before they break down the door, señor. Take me in your arms and let me see your dear face and kiss me. Then I can die with good grace, too."

"You must live—"

"Not to be sent to a foul jail, señor. And what would life be without you?"

"There is Don Diego—"

"I think of nobody but you, señor. And perhaps my death will bring home to men the treachery of the governor. Perhaps it may be of service."

Again the heavy timber struck against the door. They could hear his excellency shouting encouragement to the troopers and Sergeant Gonzales crying his orders in his loud voice.

Señor Zorro hurried to the window again and glanced out. He saw that half a dozen troopers were prepared to rush over the door the moment it was down. They would get him—but he would get some of them first! Again the ram against the door.

"It is almost the end, Señor," Señorita Lolita whispered.

"I know it, señorita."

"I can die gladly since this love has been in my life. Now—señor—your face and lips. The door—is crashing in!"

She ceased to sob and lifted her face bravely. Señor Zorro sighed, and one hand fumbled with the bottom of his mask.

But suddenly there was a commotion outside in the plaza, and the battering at the door ceased. They could hear loud voices that they had not heard before.

Señor Zorro let go of his mask and darted to the window.

CHAPTER 38

The Man Unmasked

Twenty-three horsemen were galloping into the plaza. Their horses were magnificent, their saddles and bridles were decorated with silver, their cloaks were of the finest materials, and they wore hats with plumes. Each man sat straight and proud in his saddle, his blade at his side, and every blade had a jeweled hilt.

They galloped along the face of the tavern, between the door and the soldiers who had been battering it, between the building and the governor and assembled citizens. There they turned and stood their horses side by side, facing his excellency.

"Wait! There is a better way!" their leader cried.

"Ha!" screeched the governor. "I understand. Here we have the young men of all the noble families in the southland. They have come to show their loyalty by taking this Curse of Capistrano. I thank you, caballeros. But I do not wish any of you slain by this fellow. He is not worthy of your blades, señores. Ride to one side and let my troopers deal with the rogue. Again I thank you for this show of loyalty, for this demonstration that you stand for law and order, for proper authority—"

"Peace!" their leader cried. "Your Excellency, we represent power in this section, do we not?"

"You do, caballeros," the governor said.

"Our families say who will rule, what laws are just, do they not?"

"They have great influence," the governor said.

"You would not care to stand alone against us?"

"Most assuredly not!" his excellency cried. "But I pray you, let the troopers get this fellow. It is not proper that a caballero should suffer wound or death from his blade."

"You do not seem to understand."

"Understand?" asked the governor, in a questioning tone, glancing up and down the line of mounted men.

"We have talked among ourselves, Excellency. We know our strength and power, and we have decided on certain things. Things have been done that we cannot accept. The friars of the missions have been crushed by officials. Indians have been treated worse than dogs. Even men of noble blood have been robbed because they have not been friendly to the ruling powers."

"Caballero—"

"Peace, Excellency, until I have finished. This thing came to a crisis when a gentleman and his wife and daughter were thrown into a jail by your orders. Such a thing cannot be tolerated, excellency, and so we have banded ourselves together. Be it known that we ourselves rode with this Señor Zorro when he rescued the prisoners, that we carried Don Carlos and the Doña Catalina to places of safety. We have pledged our words and honors and blades that they will not be persecuted more."

"I would say—"

"Silence, until I have finished! We stand together, and the strength of our united families is behind us. Call upon your soldiers to attack us, if you dare! Every man of noble blood up and down the length of El Camino Real would flock to our defense, would unseat you from your office, would see you humbled. We await your answer, Excellency."

"What—what do you wish?" his excellency gasped.

"First, proper consideration for Don Carlos Pulido and his family. No jail for them. If you have the courage to try them for treason, we will be on hand at the trial, and deal with any man who gives perjured testimony, and with any magistrate who does not conduct himself properly."

"Perhaps I was hasty in the matter, but I was

led to believe certain things," the governor said. "I grant you your wish. One side now, caballeros, while my men get at this rogue in the tavern."

"We are not done," their leader said. "Regarding this Señor Zorro, what has he done—actually—Excellency? Is he guilty of any treason? He has robbed no man except those who robbed the defenseless first. He has whipped a few unjust persons. He has taken sides with the persecuted, for which we honor him."

"What do you wish?"

"A complete pardon, here and now, for this man known as Señor Zorro."

"Never!" the governor cried. "He has offended me personally. He will die!" He turned around and saw Don Alejandro Vega standing near him. "Don Alejandro, you are the most influential man in this south country," he said. "You are the one man against whom even the governor dare not stand. You are a man of justice. Tell these young caballeros that what they wish cannot be granted. Tell them to return to their homes, and this show of treason will be forgotten."

"I stand behind them!" Don Alejandro thundered.

"You—you stand behind them?"

"I do, Your Excellency. I echo every word they have spoken in your presence. Persecution must cease. Grant their requests, see that your officials do right hereafter, and I give my word that there will be no treason in this southland. I will see to it myself. But oppose them, Excellency, and I will take sides against you, see you driven from office and ruined, and your foul parasites with you."

"This terrible, willful southland!" the governor cried.

"Your answer?" Don Alejandro demanded.

"I can do nothing but agree," the governor said. "But there is one thing—"

"Well!"

"I spare the man's life if he surrenders, but he must stand trial for the murder of Captain Ramón."

"Murder?" queried the leader of the caballeros, "It was a duel between gentlemen, Excellency. Señor Zorro resented an insult on the part of the commandant to the señorita."

"Ha! But Ramón was a caballero—"

"And so is Señor Zorro. He told us as much, and we believe him. So it was a duel, Excellency, and between gentlemen, according to the code. Captain Ramón was unfortunate that he was not a better man with a blade. Your answer."

"I agree," the governor said weakly. "I pardon him, and I go home to San Francisco de Asis, and persecution ceases in this locality. But I hold Don Alejandro to his promise—that there be no treason against me here if I do these things."

"I have given my word," Don Alejandro said.

The caballeros shouted their happiness and dismounted. They drove the soldiers away from the door, Sergeant Gonzales growling into his mustache because the reward had just disappeared before his eyes.

"Señor Zorro!" one cried. "Have you heard?"

"I have heard, caballero!"

"Open the door and come out—a free man!"

There was a moment's hesitation, and then the battered door was unbarred and opened. Señor Zorro stepped out with the señorita on his arm. He stopped just in front of the door, removed his sombrero and bowed low before them.

"A good day to you, caballeros!" he cried. "Sergeant, I regret that you have missed the reward, but I will see that the amount is placed to the credit of you and your men with the landlord of the tavern."

"By the saints, he is a caballero!" Gonzales cried.

"Unmask, man!" cried the governor. "I would see the face of the person who has fooled my troopers and has forced me to make a compromise."

"I fear that you will be disappointed when you see my poor features," Señor Zorro replied. "Do you expect me to look like Satan? Or can it be possible, on the other hand, that you believe I have an angelic face?"

He chuckled, glanced down at the Señorita Lolita, and then put up a hand and tore off his mask.

A chorus of gasps answered the motion, an explosive oath or two from the soldiers, cries of delight from the caballeros, and a screech of mingled pride and joy from one old gentleman.

"Don Diego, my son—my son!"

And the man before them seemed to droop suddenly in the shoulders, and sighed, and spoke in an exhausted voice.

"These are turbulent times. Can a man never meditate on music and the poets?"

And Don Diego Vega, the Curse of Capistrano, was clasped for a moment in his father's arms.

CHAPTER 39

"Meal Mush and Goat's Milk!"

They crowded forward—troopers, Indians, caballeros, surrounding Don Diego Vega and the señorita who clutched at his arm and looked up at him from proud and glistening eyes.

"Explain! Explain!" they cried.

"It began ten years ago, when I was but fifteen-years old," he said. "I heard tales of persecution. I saw my friends, the friars, annoyed and robbed. I saw soldiers beat an old Indian who was my friend. And then I decided to play this game.

"It would be a difficult game, I knew. So I pretended to have small interest in life, so that men never would connect my name with that of the highwayman I expected to become. In secret, I practiced horsemanship and learned how to handle a blade—"

"By the saints, he did," Sergeant Gonzales growled.

298

"One half of me was the worn-out Don Diego you all knew, and the other half was the Curse of Capistrano I hoped one day to be. It is a peculiar thing to explain, señores. The moment I put on the cloak and mask, the Don Diego part of me fell away. My body straightened, new blood seemed to course through my veins, my voice grew strong and firm, fire came to me! And the moment I removed cloak and mask I was the exhausted Don Diego again. Is it not a peculiar thing? I made friends with this great Sergeant Gonzales for a purpose."

"Ha! I guess the purpose, caballeros!" Gonzales cried. "Whenever this Señor Zorro was mentioned, you did not wish to hear of violence and bloodshed, but you always asked me in what direction I was going with my troopers—and you went in the other direction and did your work."

"You are an excellent guesser," said Don Diego, laughing. "I even crossed blades with you, so you would not guess I was Señor Zorro. You remember the rainy night at the tavern? I listened to your boasts, went out and put on my mask and cloak, and came in and fought you. Then I escaped, took off mask and cloak, and returned to tease with you."

"Ha!"

"I visited the Pulido hacienda as Don Diego and a short time later returned as Señor Zorro and spoke with the señorita. You almost had me,

Sergeant, that night at Friar Felipe's—the first night, I mean."

"Ha! You told me there that you had not seen Señor Zorro."

"Nor had I. The friar does not keep a mirror. The other things were not difficult, of course. You can easily understand how, as Señor Zorro, I happened to be at my own house in town when the commandant insulted the señorita.

"And the señorita must forgive me the deception. I courted her as Don Diego, and she would have none of me. Then I tried it as Señor Zorro, and the saints were kind, and she gave me her love. She turned from the wealth of Don Diego Vega to the man she loved, though she believed him an outlaw. She has showed me her true heart. Your Excellency, this señorita is to become my wife, and I hope you will think twice before you will annoy her family further."

His excellency threw out his hands in a gesture of resignation.

"And now Señor Zorro will ride no more, for there will be no need," Don Diego continued. "And besides, a married man should take some care of his life."

"And what man do I marry?" the Señorita Lolita asked, blushing.

"What man do you love?"

"I had thought that I loved Señor Zorro, but I realize now that I love the both of them," she said. "But I would rather have you Señor Zorro than the old Don Diego I knew."

"We will try to establish a perfect balance," he replied, laughing again. "I will change gradually into the man you would have me. People will say that marriage made a man of me."

He stooped and kissed her there before them all.

"Meal mush and goat's milk!" swore Sergeant Gonzales.

AFTERWORD

About the Book

If it were not for a silent film actor named Douglas Fairbanks, the character of Zorro might have disappeared shortly after Johnston McCulley created it. *The Mark of Zorro* was originally published in five installments in the late summer of 1919 in the magazine *All-Story Weekly*. It appeared under the title *The Curse of Capistrano*. Actor Douglas Fairbanks happened to read the story in the magazine while he was on his way to Europe on his honeymoon. He decided to turn *The Curse of Capistrano* into a movie named *The Mark of Zorro*.

The movie was a huge success. As a result, McCulley's story was printed as a book in 1924, under the new title, *The Mark of Zorro*. If it had not been for the movie, the character of Zorro probably would have been forgotten as soon as the last installment of *The Curse of Capistrano* had been read and the magazine thrown away. Instead, Johnston McCulley went on to write three more novels about Zorro as well as more than fifty short stories about the masked rider. In addition, there have been more than thirty films based on the character and at least six television series.

Johnston McCulley's *The Mark of Zorro* is the story that started it all. And readers still enjoy the book today. What is it about this story that continues to engage readers more than eighty-five years after it was written?

The Mark of Zorro begins with suspense. On the first page, Sergeant Gonzales declares, "It's a night for evil deeds. . . . Devils howl in the wind, and demons are in the raindrops!" And the book begins with surprises. At the end of Chapter 1, Sergeant Gonzales boasts: "'Ha! If only this brave and cunning Señor Zorro, this Curse of Capistrano, were to step through that door now—' The door suddenly was opened!" But the unexpected visitor turns out not to be the bold and dangerous Zorro but instead the gentle and harmless Don Diego Vega. Surprises like this continue throughout the book.

For many of today's readers, the biggest surprise in the book is not a surprise at all. There have been so many films and television shows based on the character that many readers know before they pick the book up that Don Diego is Zorro. But try to imagine a reader in 1919 who knew nothing about the character. It is possible that he or she would figure out Zorro's true identity from the hints given along the way. But it is also possible that such a reader would not realize the truth until the end of Chapter 38. Imagine that reader getting to this passage:

> [Señor Zorro] chuckled, glanced down at the Señorita Lolita, and then put up a hand and tore off his mask.
>
> A chorus of gasps answered the motion, an explosive oath or two from the soldiers, cries of delight from the caballeros, and a screech of mingled pride and joy from one old gentleman.
>
> "Don Diego, my son—my son!"

However, knowing Zorro's identity from the start—or figuring it out along the way—does not make the book any less interesting. For one thing, it does not take anything away from the excitement of the sword fights and the chases. For another, the reader who already knows finds pleasure in watching how slyly Don Diego creates situations that will keep people from suspecting that he is Zorro. In the first four chapters of the book, for example, he appears in the tavern first as Don Diego, then as Zorro, and a few minutes later as Don Diego again. It is fun to watch Don Diego goad Sergeant Gonzales (with the sergeant's own words) about his encounter with Zorro, knowing full well exactly what happened: "You promised me . . . that you would tell me the whole thing, word by word. Did he not say so, landlord? You declared that you would relate how you played with him; how you laughed at him while you fought; how you pressed him back after a time and then ran him through—"

Scenes such as this one also illustrate another element that makes *The Mark of Zorro* so enjoyable—humor. Much of the humor comes from Sergeant Gonzales's exaggerated claims of what he will do to Zorro or his imaginative explanations of how Zorro defeated him and escaped. Knowing the truth, the reader can enjoy the sergeant's bragging attempts to cover up his failures with lies. He says on several occasions that Zorro escaped because he had a gang of ten or twenty men. Notice the sergeant's surprise when his lies seem to have come true: "Sergeant Gonzales rubbed his eyes with the back of one hand and swore softly that he had been taking too much wine. He had lied so often about Señor Zorro having a band of men, that here was the band materialized out of his falsehoods."

Another source of humor is Don Diego's feeble attempt to win Señorita Lolita. He would prefer to jump directly from asking for permission to court her to being told what time to show up for the wedding. He offers to send his servant to serenade the señorita: "I have a servant who plays the guitar wonderfully. . . . Tonight I will order him to come out and play beneath the señorita's window." Lolita's poor parents are shocked at such an idea. Only when Don Diego's own father threatens to cut off his inheritance does the young man reluctantly agree to attempt to court the woman properly. Don Carlos and his wife are relieved at this change. But once Don Diego begins to play and sing, they have second thoughts:

> **Don Diego [was] playing his guitar and singing a verse of a song that had to do with bright eyes and love. Don Carlos and his wife glanced at each other again, this time in apprehension. They wished that he would stop, for he was not much of a musician or vocalist, and they feared that he might lose what ground he had gained in the señorita's estimation.**

The surprises and the humor are important aspects in making the book appealing. But even more important is the character of Don Diego/Zorro. Zorro is mysterious and elusive. At times, he seems to have almost supernatural powers. At the beginning of Chapter 2, we are expecting Zorro to appear. The door of the tavern suddenly opens: "In came a gust of wind and rain and a man with it. The candles flickered, and one went out." But it turns out not to be Zorro. At the end of Chapter 2, the pattern is repeated. Will it be Zorro this time? "And again the door was opened suddenly, and a man entered the inn on a gust of the storm." After Zorro humiliates Sergeant Gonzales in Chapter 4, he leaps from the tavern window and seems to vanish into thin air:

> **In rushed the wind and rain, and the candles went out.**
> **—and no man could tell in what direction.**

This mysterious masked swordsman appears when least expected and then disappears without a trace. In Chapter 9 when Captain Ramón arrives at Don Carlos Pulido's hacienda, we believe that Zorro has ridden away, pursued by the soldiers. To the surprise of Ramón and the reader, Zorro leaps out of a closet in Don Carlos's living room. And in Chapter 17, when Sergeant Gonzales and his men are chasing Zorro, it seems as if the bandit has gone to Friar Felipe's hacienda for safety. But when the sergeant and his men search the place, the only outsider they can find is Don Diego. Once again, Zorro seems to have vanished. If we do not know that Zorro and Don Diego are the same person, we are as mystified as the sergeant is.

At first glance, Zorro seems like the perfect hero. He is sly and clever. He is a skilled swordsman and horseman. He is daring. He is a gentleman. But he is not perfect. He is a human being, not a superhero. Sometimes he makes mistakes. In Chapter 15, Zorro burns Captain Ramón's letter to the governor and warns him: "Let me not hear of you sending any letter similar to the one I have just destroyed." But he does not realize that he has burned only a copy of the letter and that the original is already on its way to the governor.

In Chapter 35, he makes a miscalculation that almost costs him his life. After killing Captain Ramón, he rushes outside to his horse. As he does so, he realizes his mistake: "The dawn had come. . . . Señor Zorro had delayed too long with the governor and commandant. He swung into his saddle and urged his beast out of the patio—and then a full realization of his peril came to him." Ultimately, this mistake puts him into a situation from which he cannot escape. He and Lolita end up barricaded in the tavern with no way out. It is only a matter of moments until the soldiers will burst through the door and kill him. Unlike a superhero, who can get out of any situation, Zorro survives only because the caballeros step in.

At first, this may seem disappointing. Here the great Señor Zorro has to be rescued by a group of ordinary gentlemen. In fact, this is the important point about the book. Zorro is an ordinary man who fights an unjust government. What *is* extraordinary about him is that he is able to inspire others to take responsibility. The caballeros no longer need Zorro telling them what must be done. Zorro proves himself to be the best kind of leader—a leader who makes leaders of others, a leader who enables others to live up to their full potential.

In the process of doing this, he also enables himself to live up to his full potential by making Don Diego a complete person. Up until he reveals his identity, he has been living a dual existence. One side of him has been the energetic outlaw, the man of action, the exciting lover, the man who fights injustice. The other side has been the always exhausted, practical, boring rich-man's son. Don Diego himself is amazed at how he has been affected by the two different roles. As he explains in Chapter 29:

> One half of me was the worn-out Don Diego you all knew, and the other half was the Curse of Capistrano I hoped one day to be. It is a peculiar thing to explain, señores. The moment I put on the cloak and mask, the Don Diego part of me fell away. My body straightened, new blood seemed to course through my veins, my voice grew strong and firm, fire came to me! And the moment I removed cloak and mask I was the exhausted Don Diego again. Is it not a peculiar thing?

While divided, neither part of the man can live a complete life. As Zorro, he does important work in fighting injustice. But he is also in constant danger. As Don Diego, he learns useful information that helps Zorro succeed. But he is not able to accomplish much. He is not even able to convince Lolita to marry him. In the end, he looks to bring together the best qualities of the two parts. When Lolita says that she now realizes that she loves both Zorro and Don Diego, he replies: "We will try to establish a perfect balance. . . . I will change gradually into the man you would have me. People will say that marriage made a man of me." Once Zorro removes his mask, he and Don Diego can become one.

However, he is not able to remove his mask and become a whole person until the world around him has been made whole. At the beginning of *The Mark of Zorro*, people are suffering under an unjust government. Good families are having their money and property confiscated. Honest and hard-working people are being punished for crimes they did not commit. Decent people are being beaten because the people in power feel like beating them. Even nature echoes the unsettled conditions of the time. As Chapter 1 opens, sheets of rain beat down in the night and the wind shrieks "like a soul in torment."

By contrast, the weather conditions at the end of the book are greatly improved. The sun has risen. The plaza is "bathed in brilliance." There is "no mist, no fog in the hills even." And, by the end of the book, the unjust government has been brought under control. The governor has agreed to drop all charges against the Pulido family and against Zorro. And he has agreed to see that "persecution ceases in this locality." The governor is not a changed man. He will go back to his "foul parasites" in San Francisco de Asis. But at least in this part of the country, where the caballeros have stood up to him, he will no longer persecute people.

The only reason the governor backs down is that the caballeros have united against him. When Zorro was acting alone, the governor had the potential to overcome him. The oppression stops because the caballeros find the courage to stand up to injustice. Without their action, Zorro would have been killed by the soldiers and the world would have continued as it had been. The change starts with one man being willing to stand up for what is right. But he cannot succeed alone. Others must follow his leadership—and become leaders themselves.

This, then, is the message of *The Mark of Zorro*. Each individual must have the courage to stand up for what is right and just. Each individual must encourage others to do the same. Only then will we live in a safe, unified world, at peace with others and ourselves. And only then can each of us live up to our potential as a complete human being.